Library of Congress

Gardner, Taniesha
       Figurines Dancing in my Head; A memoir/Nicci Gardner.
ISBN: 978-0-578-71241-3
TXu2203396 2020

Figurines Dancing in My Head

A Memoir

Nicci Gardner

Table of Contents

Introduction

I wrote this book as a testament of the goodness of God and how He specializes in reconstructing anyone who asks for a new life. I am sharing my diary as evidence of His unfailing love and the patience He showed me. I pray that as You read it, you will be able to see my slow personal and spiritual growth. Over the years, I always had it in the back of my mind that one day I would publish these memoirs, but fear and embarrassment always held me back—until recently; the Spirit kept reminding me of these old entries, and God led me to share them with You.

> *Sing to the Lord; praise his name. Each day proclaim the good news that he saves. Publish his glorious deeds among the nations. Tell everyone about the amazing things he does. Great is the Lord! He is most worthy of praise! He is to be feared above all gods.*
>
> —Psalm 96:2-4

My prayer is that You are blessed and that You can see how God has restored unto me that which the Devil meant to devour. If You have a wayward child, sister, brother, mom, dad, friend, or any

4

loved one, please continue to pray for them and watch God work on them the way

he did on me. If by chance You want a change and want to know how to be a Christian, and where to start as a believer of the Almighty God, read my journey and be inspired. God doesn't require us to be perfect for

Him to love us; He just wants us to open our hearts to start wanting Him. He saw me at my worst, but He still had a plan for me. To God be the glory. Be blessed.

Love,
Nicci

Acknowledgements

I did my best,

my best is good enough,

and God will bridge the gap.

CHAPTER ONE

÷

Teenage Doom and Gloom

The room was dim, and I had fallen asleep with the television on. Something stirred me from my slumber. It was a hand—down my pants. This had happened before, but this time was different. I knew who it was. As he fumbled with my bottom, I pretended to be asleep. My body was stiff, and, in my six-year-old mind, I thought he would stop if I pretended to be asleep. My heart was beating wildly, and my mind was racing. My mind raced—*what is going on? what is happening?* I didn't know what to do or how to react. I just knew that something bad was happening in that moment. The spirit of fear entered my body and consumed me. My chest was hurting. My heart was about to burst right out of my body. I don't remember much after that, but one thing that always stuck with me was not the act itself—it was the fear. Fear, anxiety and depression stuck on me like white on rice ever since my childhood, accompanied by paranoia. For the next twenty years, I battled a lack of confidence, an inability to trust others, and low self-esteem.

***

The preacher was telling a story of the Prodigal Son. As I sat in the congregation, I listened intently. The story resonated with my nine-year-old self. I was a prodigal. I needed to come back to God. During an intense alter call, I leaned over my friend, Nicky. I proposed to her that if she would go up, I would go up too. I didn't want to be by myself, and Nicky was easy to coerce into anything. She agreed as I hoped, and up we went for a call to baptism. The pastor asked us a few questions, and I knew he wanted to gauge our understanding of what we were doing. Our answers must have satisfied him because, the next thing we knew, the deaconesses were helping us get dressed in white robes. I was in the big pool, and the water was up to my chest.

"Do you accept God as your Lord and Savior?" I nodded. "I now baptize you in the name of the Father, Son and Holy Ghost." My dad covered my eyes with a white rag and down my body went into this 'watery grave.' I came up and looked around. I suddenly felt different. I felt clean. I felt new—like a whole different person new. There aren't any words I can place together in the English language that describe how I felt after that.

Middle school was very different from elementary. I was eleven in the sixth grade. It was in January, on a Wednesday to be exact, after gym class when the unthinkable happened: I got my period. I was both in shock and weirded out at the same time. Some of my friends had gotten theirs and talked about it sometimes, but I didn't expect this now. So, I stuffed some bathroom tissue where it needed to be and continued life. Over the next few months, I threw away sheets, underwear and pants to hide the evidence. Seeing all that blood used to freak me out and give me anxiety. I needed help, but who could I turn to? One weekend afternoon, my mom was napping in her room. I stood next to the bed nervously with my head down. "Hey, Mom?" I began. I was trying to find the words to tell her I needed help and I was ashamed. "How are you doing?" I asked. She ignored me. "Um, you okay?" I continued, trying to get her to ask me if I was okay too;

but she didn't. She began to yell and scream at me to leave her alone, and that she needed a nap. I usually did not bother or follow her around, and I was embarrassed; so, I left.

My mom didn't always act like that. On one occasion, I remember her attending a parent-teacher meeting. Mom and I sat at the table with my teachers and another assistant. They told her how I struggled academically, didn't turn in my homework, performed poorly on tests, and bullied my peers. They added that I would benefit from having a resource class once a day to help me learn better, and they advised her that I also needed a speech therapist. I wasn't aware I had a speech impediment. I knew I stuttered at times and was teased for it, but I didn't know my teachers had difficulty communicating with me. During the meeting, my head hung low; my spirit was crushed, and I fought back tears. Mom and I exited the meeting and, when we got in the hallway, she embraced me and told me everything was going to be alright. My bottled-up emotions burst out, and I began sobbing uncontrollably. In my heart, I wanted to do better. I also remember her going on a weekend band field trip with my friends and me. She acted like the other regular moms, and I was proud to have my friends see her. It was different having so much attention from her, but I liked it and didn't want the weekend to end.

She and my father got into an argument some months later, and she and I left for the grocery store right after. I kept looking at her and asking myself why she was acting so weird. She couldn't focus her eyes, her speech was slurred, and she kept falling asleep. Up and down the aisles we went as she filled the cart with random items. My small questions were ignored, and people in the store were following us and asking her if she was okay. I was confused. At the checkout counter, she couldn't find her money. We had to leave our things there, and the manager escorted my mom to the door. He told me to make sure she got some rest. I was scared to have her drive, but I was just twelve and did what she said. After an hour of dangerous driving with her struggling to stay awake behind the wheel, we ended up in a parking lot. She fell asleep in the driver's seat. I, on the other hand, couldn't sleep; I just kept staring out the window. With the car off, it was chilly. For the next two days we went from one person's house to another. Her behavior was erratic. Usually, I had to stay in the car.

Yes, I am a millennial. Back in the 80s, Nancy Regan came up with a slogan that was all over television and billboards, and it also managed to infiltrate the elementary school system I attended— "Just Say No." The war on drugs was a serious issue for the nation as a whole; we needed an intervention and fast. But being so young, even though I heard and saw it, registering the vastness of the problem didn't resonate for me until it was at my front door.

The crack epidemic left children, women, men, and families in complete disarray. Just in case you are not familiar with what crack is, it is a cheap, highly addictive form of cocaine. Because of its popularity and price, the number of Americans who became addicted jumped from 4.2 to 5.8 million in 1985 alone. This epidemic devastated our African American communities and us as a people. Crime and incarceration rates of our people soared remarkably in the 1980s.

I was thirteen. My mom had asked if I wanted to ride with her to her friend's house. My mom and I didn't have a relationship, but anytime she asked me to do something, I would say yes, hoping that my work would produce a love for me in her. We rode to her friend's house, and I didn't know this lady. I'd never seen her before, and she had two small children—a girl and a boy. We all rode in the same vehicle, and the two women dropped us kids off at Chuck E. Cheese's. My mom handed me two twenty-dollar bills, and they left. In my heart, I knew I wasn't going to see her for a few days. We had been at Chuck E, Cheese's for several hours, and it was closing time. I tried multiple times to call her cell, but she would not answer. I called my dad, who was an hour away. He said he was coming. The place was closed by then, so the two small kids and I were waiting outside in the Alaskan cold. Eventually, my dad showed up and took us back to our house.

As a young teenager, I loved watching Michael Jackson on MTV; and he had just released some new music videos. I was in my room with my headphones on when my brother barged in telling me Mom was trying to kill herself, that I needed to come quick. He led me to the garage where I found her tying her robe tie around her neck, standing on a stool, fastening it to the garage door frame. My siblings were crying and pleading with her. I came, I saw, I left and went back to my room to finish listening to the HiStory album. During tough times at home, I would always resort to my room—reading and listening to music. This evening was no different from the rest. My dad came in, telling me to talk to Mom. She followed him into my room and snatched off my headphones. She sat on my bed, crying, rocking, and slobbering on herself. I remember feeling indifferent. The mental image of her became fixed in my mind. I remained speechless. I just stared at her.

It was wintertime and cold outside. A thick layer of snow covered the ground, a foot or maybe even two. No one was home except us kids. My dad was at work and Mom was out binging again. My younger siblings and I were watching television when I heard some shuffling on the deck followed by some firm knocks at the door. I peered out the blinds to see a police car and two other cars I didn't recognize. I was looking for my mom in the back seat of one of them, but I didn't find her. They were social workers, coming to take my brothers and sisters and me into foster care. They had interviewed us before, and I knew they would be back. They tried the door. It was locked. I got scared that they would force their way in and take us all to different homes, and I wouldn't see my siblings again. With my baby brother wrapped in a blanket, my other two brothers and sister and I snuck out a back window, into the woods. Down a trail we went, and we stayed in hiding. It was cold and our limbs were getting numb. I told everyone to be quiet and not make a sound. The officer and social workers stayed in the driveway, trying the door for about thirty minutes. When they finally left, I was relieved. We snuck back in the house through that same window. A notice was stuck to the front door, and I balled it up and threw it in the trash can. I thought to myself, "A close call."

During my last year of high school, we moved way out in the middle of nowhere it seemed. I was at the house with my younger siblings trying to make something for us to eat. We didn't have any groceries—just some odds and ends we found in the pantry. The phone rang, and it was Mom. I hadn't heard from her in about a week, and she asked if I would come get her at the grocery store. The only vehicle we had was the U-Haul truck we were using to move, so I told her I would be there in about fifteen minutes. During the drive, all I could think of was the sound in her voice. She sounded scared and secretive. As I pulled into the parking lot, I saw my mom on the sidewalk of the entrance to the store. Her head was down, and she quickly jumped in the truck and put her head down towards the floorboards. I got scared. I asked her what was wrong and why she was hiding. She said, "Just drive!" On the way back home, I noticed a silver Honda following us. I knew what the problem was, as usual. She probably got fronted some drugs, she told the drug people that I was going to bring money to pay them back, and she lied to them and assumed we could outdrive these people. I glanced at the gas tank, and we were in desperate need of gas, so I pulled into the nearest service station. She stayed in hiding. All I had was seven dollars in my pocket, so I put it in the tank. As I was pumping, the Honda pulled up behind us and one of the people got out and started telling me what they wanted from my mom. But I already knew. The woman acted like she wanted to fight, and I had the gas nozzle in my hand. The station was very busy, and she seemed hesitant to escalate. The man driving was cursing at me and towards my mom's side of the truck. I told the woman that if she came any closer, I was going to shower her in unleaded eighty-seven. I got back in the U-Haul truck and drove off towards home again. They continued following us. As I was looking in the rearview mirror, all I could think of was my three younger brothers and sister who were at home waiting for me to return. My youngest brother was two at the time, and he was my favorite. He slept with me and always followed me around. He liked it when I played with his matchbox cars. Anger kindled within my loins and turned to rage, and I glanced in the rearview mirror again to see the silver Honda. My mom was silent. Still driving, I suddenly halted the truck in the middle a two-lane highway and put it in Park. People were beeping and honking at me, but I didn't care. Searching under the seats, I found a crowbar. I got out of the truck and headed towards the Honda with the crowbar in my hand. I swung the weapon and struck the hood of the car. I was cursing, yelling and demanding all of them to get out and say those same things to me they had been saying at the gas station. They wouldn't budge, but just stared at me blankly. In the end, they stopped following us, and we returned home without them. I was seventeen.

August 1997

Bill collectors…phone, stop ringing…I can't take the noise. Never-land searching for homeless child because I am in need. Don't let greed overcome and destroy you. Kingdom, I'm waiting please take me home. Trouble is near, danger is here. Quiet! Tinker bell rock with me, Gladys sing for me. Someone praises me. Heart has beat; brain is capable; bones in body are broken. To stomp on me, death shall overcome. Lord Jesus Savior, rescue me for I have scraped my knee. Pluck my burdens away. Healing hand, touch me in life. Unknown person captures me, and let me join your world, for thou aren't accepted in this one.

I have a lot of doubts; miserable. Ongoing circus cruise rides, dazzling and shining galaxies, talking hill tops and echoing gas chambers. Fantasies of joy surrounded by guilt and frustration. This non-respected person has been made a long-time laughingstock for too long. Merry-go-around, please end. Money is nothing but to open doors for wishing on stars is spectacular. Love is the key, but evil is my stop sign. Even though I try to cover wounds, blood soaks up everything. Bloody tears when sleeping souls. There is a journey for each person being a victim of never-ending dreams of friendships;

friendships will always linger around through life. Please, help me because I'm deteriorating day by day.

Birds, snakes, rodents have been lost. I didn't mean to slaughter; why bother when all one's hopes are animal friendships. Guardians, please lend a hand; the fires and depths of hell are looming. Save me because I'm falling. I'm tired of being put down and slapped around; I know I'm not a rag doll. Mary Poppins, Mr. Rogers if I die, will you remember me? Beauty lurking around varieties of corners find me. Lost children, Peter Pan, may I join? Racial slurs, I'm tired! Please, my self-esteem is leaking. Friends are sharks; blood in water. If I drown, will you save me?

Yelling, screaming, power...hand BANG...hurts like fire following a red face. Alleys, homeless humans, I'm sensitive to your pain, but I can't heal you if I can't heal myself. Wind, I beg of you blow my sorrow away; I beg let not me be alone in this horrifying world. Hold my hand; lead me and let me stand. Tongues are greater than fists. Believe; freaks; Merrick, I love you. All dogs beware; teeth don't hurt, words do. Near prostitute; in future if I slip, will you grab me? Sunset don't leave, bring joy to all one's desperate needs. Don't leave me, precious. I don't like to be left alone; cover my nudity. Door mat, please don't grow old.

If so, dream lover come rescue me. A green plant is rotting; please get better. Mom, Dad be smart; don't leave for they may never find me again. Drugs, alcohol, estranged families, fragileness overcome thee. There is no time for departing; I know I can win a war. Nanna do not sicken. Marie, find my missing dreams. I will never accomplish anything. Help; give me your hand. Window, let me see through the future; will I make it another hour? If I shall die, will I burn? I am ugly, stupid; help me. I am not of any brilliance; my aching pains burn daily. A question to God: May I, God, generate into another creature besides this one?

Suffering is all over the world. Suffering and sadness are decaying me. I try very hard to go on with my losing life; I guess you know how I feel. I say to my siblings I want something else, then eventually I get it; but it isn't what I want. Every day I consider the mirror, and I see an ugly reflection staring at me. I'm disgusted with myself. Believe it or not, every little tease hurts. What about you? I'm misunderstood a lot by my parents. I listen to music because I can escape into another person and just zap my chains away. I feel like an alien being kept in bondage. My freedom will never come, will it?

Treasures, jewels, and riches have been brought and taken from my personality. Meanness, cruelty and depression have taken their toll. Uselessness is my body weight. Colors of cultures don't excite me. Grades aren't my identity. Selfishness is a bizarre fantasy, smothered by false words. Love and affection are needed. I am sleeping with vipers; save me. If I shall give affection, will I get it back? I die, every day. God, are You real? If so, prove Your existence. May I touch thee? God, why me? My world is falling. Walls around me are caving. What is my purpose? Do You love me? Where is my sign? My aching pain is pulling me down; my insides hurt...so much pain. I'm going to drop! I'm falling. PLEASE! My soul is burning.

November 1997

Solitude

My solitude has been so invaded with the intentions of complete ignorance. My solitude. Are my wishes others' exaggerations seem to distant from reality? My solitude.

The Pretty Lady (Part 1)

As the sex machine of the city walked by, people cheering, men whistling. The movement of the hips and the flowing of the hair, the unforgettable batting of the eyelashes. The gorgeous woman walked swiftly down the street like a bright moon in a black box. Underneath the diamonds, rubies, and pearls was a scared innocent little girl that all she saw was cruelty. She looked to her left, then right. Nothing but an aching heart was brought upon her spirit. Then greed came up eating a piece of fresh bread and asked, "Are you going to eat that?" The little girl looked sadly into greed's eyes and started gushing out tears, not just any tears. Bloody tears.

As the innocent little girls' eyes arose from their home spot upon the ground, bloody tears filled her eyes and slowly ran down her light tan skin on her face. Full of weariness and sorrow that shall scar her personality for a lifetime sentence. The little girl fell on her knees, giving up and continued her unforgettable weeping. Answerless, Greed disappeared. Suddenly a bright light shone over the human sparrow. Unable to be surprised, the fragile girl looked up into the bright light to find a glowing dove that was carrying a perfect rose that was grasped between its spotless beak. Shaking. Afraid of violence, the little girl's hand reached out, full of bruises. She gently removed the so perfect rose. As soon as the rose hit her possession, it turned dull; no more glowing, no more sparkling, just dull. The little girl broke down once more to express her feelings. A man with long hair softly tapped her on the shoulder; paralyzed with fear, the girl, not knowing who it was, took off running. "Why run, my child? thou heareth your cries thou seeketh no harm?" Then the pretty lady awoke from her dream to find an odd-looking man in her bedroom. Not afraid of this matter, the whore stood up to find that same man glancing down upon her. Both began staring at each other. Questions? Answers? Nothing.

January 2, 1999

I'm Ugly

I'm so ugly I could hide. I've never had any pride. My face is full of scars. I wish I were one of the stars. My hair is falling out; all I do is pout. How many times have I told you I'm just like you too? Why can't I be A-class, but I would never pass.

January 23, 1999

As a child, I used to love God so much. I worshipped him always. But what is wrong with me now? Life just is not going my way. Can anything make me happy? Jesus, when will I find You again? I want this recess to end. I feel like an outcast, a reject from society, God; can I please get ahead in life? Or shall I end it with a knife? Without a reason, I've seemed to have committed treason. What will my future bring me? Life is not a cup of tea. I live in a fantasy land; people think I have dirty hands. What's wrong? My life is a bomb.

August 11, 1999

I hate you! You make my life miserable! I despise your disappointments! You are the cause of my depression. No one in the world hurts me like you do. I hate you. You tear down my self-esteem. You make it hard for me to make friends. You put me down and cause frustration. If you were gone, my life would change. I hate you. You, disappointment! I'm on the edge, and you're pushing me. Disappointment, I hate you! Look at me, Disappointment! Don't you see my tears, Disappointment? I'm nothing; I'm a loser.

Disappointment! Quit pushing me. One day I will jump. I'll jump you, Disappointment! I hate you! You're nothing but disappointing trash!!! My despair is the cause of you, I hate you hate you hate you hate you hate you hate you hate you. You, Disappointment. Look at me! Look at me! I'm not your maid! Don't make my decisions; don't give me options. I hate you, Disappointment! You, Disappointment! I'm dying, deteriorating; are you happy? I hate you! You tear me down constantly. Can't you see I'm dying? Will you care? I'm breaking down, do you care? I hate you! Disappointment!

November 25, 1999

Dear Journal,

Help me. Help me. Someone help me. Listen, I'm 17 years old. Okay, do you know how I feel? I feel sick. I hate xx. I'd rather have xx than be stuck with xx. If I ever sit down and talk to him, this is what I'd say. My suicide note:

To whoever cares, I'm dead now and you can't bring me back. I hope you hurt just a little bit. You have made me cry on dozens of occasions. Listen, I have no friends, and I can't socialize. What's

25

wrong with me? It's you, you know, by your tongue, I lay here. I hate you. I hate you. You're a disappointment that makes my life horrible. Well, I'm dead now. It feels so good. You can't yell at me now, can you, disappointment? I'm heartbroken. I hurt. You think I'm dirty? You think I'm selfish? You appreciate nothing. Jesus, where are You? I've been patient, I've tried. You said You'd never leave me; I'm alone. Please help me. Look, I'm somebody! Look, Disappointment, I have dreams. You cannot take them from me. Or can you?

CHAPTER TWO

÷Sugar Me Blue

An education was my only way out of the house and into a more positive life. Since my sophomore year in high school, the idea of going to college became a goal that I strived for. Now it was getting closer, and I was about a year out. I started working at Taco Bell and Toys R Us. I also took little odd jobs like babysitting and hair braiding. My money was growing, and I was proud of myself. I even had a checkbook, savings account, and a little credit card. For safe keeping, I had a small piggy bank hidden in my room with some small petty cash for emergency purposes. I felt independent, and I was sure

I'd have enough or close to enough to get me started in a new place. Until I was robbed.

Coming home from school, in my room, my small piggy bank had been ransacked; it lay across my bed with a screwdriver resting next to it. The only thing left was a few pennies strewn about my comforter. My heart sank, and she came in my room with a face full of fury demanding we go to the bank and I give her $500. I refused. The argument followed me outside while I was trying to leave. By then her drug friend, Lisa, was in her red car waiting on her in front of the house. She then grabbed me by my shirt and slammed my body into the garage door. She continued cursing and slapping me. I held my ground, and she wrapped her hand around my ponytail. By this time, her friend Lisa got out and told her to come on. She finally left.

November 2000

I'm only human, brought forth by a woman. I'm less than dirt and full of hurt. But You have a plan for me? That will last through history. Why do You answer me? My every little plea. I have changed so much, you, see? A long way from poverty. But You have a plan for me? That will last through eternity?

Saturday January 5, 2001

Astrologers say, something is on way. He's going to come thru Orion's belt. His love often felt. Triumphant angels singing majestic melodies and trumpets will sound when that day comes around. A magnificent kingdom they call the New Jerusalem will descend, for some, too late to amend. Gems, stones, and precious metals are the material used to make this utopia. Angels harmonize with the natural sounds of nature. I hear beautiful voices give praises as rushing waters roar with sheer delight. Elephants, lions, birds, and insects align themselves and, with perfection, Heaven 's orchestra has a celebration for this joyous occasion. Captured by this large production, I sit and listen. In my own thought, I plot…You did this for me? Indeed, it's true. The clouds rolled back with a hue.

February 22, 2001

There are so many things that I need to learn about You. When I start my prayer, should I ask for forgiveness or should I come to You first with thanksgiving? Oh, well, I guess a prayer is a prayer. I'm going to drop my prayers, frustrations, requests, and cries at Your feet. Please, grant me knowledge and wisdom so that I can apply to my academics. You already know that I need a 3.3 GPA to be in the nursing program next semester. It is so crucial that I obtain this. God, You have done so much with so little for so long. I give You my current 2.31 GPA. I ask that You turn that into 3.31 and give it back to me. You have answered so many of my prayers. I'm so discouraged right now. Satan is beating me up unmercifully. I've been studying for A&P and Micro. But I keep failing my tests. Where am I going wrong? Is this a sign from You to me? Bless those who do me wrong and say evil things to and against me. God give me the fruits of the Spirit. Help me when I can't help myself. Open a window for me when Satan has closed all the doors. Father, You know I owe 30% more on my tuition. Bless me so that I can rid myself of that burden. God, I need a plan for this summer. Help me to get on my feet and be independent. I know my parents have 4 other kids, so help me to get a nursing scholarship. Just so I can support myself. In the future, help me to apply You to my occupation so that I can be a witness for You. God, I pray for my family. I pray that they will safely be relocated to Anchorage in a big house. I pray for my brother Derek Jr. I pray that You continuously heal him spiritually, mentally, physically, and emotionally. I pray for my brother Jahne'. I pray for You to heal him of his mental conditions and that the hole in his brain will be deleted and that he experiences joy, love, peace, and understanding in life. I pray for my little sister Tia Rosa. I pray that she will have a closer relationship with You. I pray that You will use her as a vessel to witness for You to others. I pray for her to be able to have a bright future. I also pray for my littlest brother Dresen Joseph. I pray that You raise him in the path of salvation and bless his little heart. God, I pray for my family's salvation, as well as my own. When I enter the pearly gates of Heaven, I want to see the beautiful faces of my beloved family. When You open the gates of Heaven and call my name, "Nicci, come forth," I want to see the faces of my family. Thank You for being my shelter in the storm; thank You for being my friend when no other would listen. Thank You for allowing me to go home for Christmas. Thank You for hearing my humble cries. Thank You for the good grades as well as the bad ones. Thank You for my shoes, clothes, food, friends, parents, and siblings. Thank You for giving me a future, a new start on life. Thank You for my health. God, help me to have a closer relationship with You. Today, give me sensitive eyes and ears. Make me calm. Give me guidance. Grant me safety on my way today; give me energy and make me strong. Father, give me a rich blessing from You today. Be with me and make me an instrument for You so that I may witness to others about your wondrous beauty. Help me to be able to graduate in 3 to 4 years.

August 23, 2001

I forgot to pray to You this morning. Please, forgive me. God, I've got so much to say and ask of You. I've never felt this way before. Isaiah the prophet says that You have a plan for me. What is it? I get so confused sometimes. You know this, right? Why do You have me going thru this all the time? Why do I hurt constantly? From the morning when I awake to the evening when I lay down. How long will I hurt? You know the past, present, and the future. Will You send someone or something to cheer me up? Oh, well. For the past couple of months, I've cried, shouted, and screamed to You. All this time, You planned something for me. Right? I wonder, why do You leave me going through this? Is this the Job test that I asked for? Is it? If it is, please take it away. All that time, I thought I was doing right by You. I planted your laws and morals in my head; they stayed. Now, I feel that they have backfired against me.

October 30, 2001

It's as if something is wrong with me,

Just getting over a catastrophe,

A prisoner of my own love for he,

Who hurt me bad, emotionally

Now, solo, awkward to utter hello

…I'm lonely…

An admired outcast of society

Plagued by depression and beauty

Trying to avoid a crowd

Too weak to say it out loud

…I'm lonely…

Thoughts of fantasy aren't my reality

God's creation of simplicity

Confused prayer warrior

With the imagination of horror

Hidden pain is my companion

Always feeling abandoned

…I'm lonely…

Low self-esteem wants to conquer me

I cannot seem to win, You see.

Been this way for years

Shedding so many tears

…I'm lonely…somebody…help me….

November 2001

Constantly, thoughts of you run rampant in my mind. Distortion is my penalty for not seeing through your false, deeply religious nature. I need to let go. Now, I realize my future designation has been slaughtered by artificial love. My mind suffered a mental catastrophe. I need to let go. My delusional fantasies never will be my reality. This conviction has terminated my understanding. Asphyxiated in my own thought, I'm brutalized. I need to let go.

November 3, 2001

My Father

Even though this would might try to hold me down, my Father in Heaven is always around. He said He's got a plan for me, that'll last through eternity. An awaiting crown of gold and a robe of white. A trophy for my long fight. To stay by His side and not hide His peaceful lovingkindness and everlasting understanding. He's said He'd wash me as white as snow and never let me go. Well, touch me and make me new, and I will tell you by who.

Monday, November 26, 2001

SS–

For some reason, I keep thinking about this past Saturday afternoon. Why? I just don't understand why you dropped off my plant at my grandparents' house. Especially the aloe vera, which was well, alive and flourishing. I have doubts concerning it being the same plant I gave to you May 1, 2001. The soil seems different from the original soil I had planted it in. Fortunately, every time I look at the window, I see it. Subsequently I think of all the thing you said and promised and done to me. That plant represented us, our relationship. How dare you let it turn beautiful and leave it on a doorstep? I've come to expect this sort of thing from you. I still wonder were you trying to be evil or kind. At this moment in time, I look at it as you are being mean and rubbing something in my face. About an hour ago, I saw you driving past me. You had someone in your car. I think I looked twice, just to see Quincy's bald head. What a relief. My day would have been weird if it was some chick. I try my best to keep dudes away. I try hard not to be seen with the same guy twice. I try to avoid you as much as possible. I know I promised myself a million times that I wouldn't write you anymore "invisible" letters. But I can't help it. Gradually, it's wearing off. I started liking this other guy. I've liked him for about 2 ½ months now. I compare the two of you all the time. It's different. I've never been physically attracted to you. But I think he's cute! Oh, well, once things gear up between us, hopefully you'll be a completely closed chapter. Merely forgotten.

November 31, 2001

Gawking sounds, beaming lights, and flashing cameras. Sparkling diamonds, tight satin clothes, polished nails, and dazzling hair. Uncomprehensive beauty. A prideful stride with an A-class ride and an angelic beau by my side. Uncomprehensive beauty…I'm blessed. I've come too far from where I started from.

December 6, 2001

Dear Journal,

I can't believe what happened yesterday. Or even today. Monique and I were studying for Statistics in the library at about 1:15pm. I looked up and saw my ever-rude ex-boyfriend, Shawn. Suddenly he turned around before entering the foyer of the library. I figured he saw me and bolted. I must admit that I was kind of hurt, but I am like so used to it by now. Oh, well, I thought. Later, he walked in. I kept trying to look away and act like I didn't see him, but he kept coming closer to the study room I was in! His actions so surprised me. Usually, he just ignores me. He politely came in and said to Monique and me, "Excuse me, I'm sorry to interrupt, but, Nicci, can I speak with you for moment?" Nervously, I looked around as if I needed approval from the walls or something. In return, I got up and walked towards him. I honestly don't remember everything he said to me, but I remember a couple things that stick out in my mind and sort of confused me slightly. Phrases like the following, but I didn't understand:

S: I'm on the rebound right now. (From who? Me?)

S: I'm cool now. (What were you before?)

S: I had to deal with some stuff. (What stuff?)

S: Some stuff you just can't throw away. (Like what?)

Anyway, I thank God he finally talked to me yesterday; he also said hi to me today. I just remembered last year this same day I was writing a letter about him. It is awfully funny how things happen sometimes. I keep wondering about what's going to happen between us. I love him so much. (Don't tell anybody!) I wonder what he feels and thinks about the whole situation. I'm not sure. For some reason, his sister is friendly with me. I miss him dearly. I just remembered my daddy saying, "Separation causes appreciation." It's true. I'm not sure where our future is going to lead. I just put it in God's hands. For not my will, but thine be done. Another thing I want to tell you about is MS (we'll call him that for now). I've liked him since like September, but he's so special. He finds so much fault in me. I tend to get uncomfortable around him. He's also shady. He can carry on a perfect conversation with my friends, but when it comes to me, it's dumb stuff. Like chit chat and tea sipping. He keeps mentioning his ex-girl. I always compare him to my ex-dude. I know I need to stop, but I can't help it. They both have equally good and bad qualities. But I have a lot more feelings for "2bit" than I do for Mr. Chocolate Skin.

Lovingly yours, Me

December 9, 2001

Dear Journal,

I'm going try to talk to you at least once per day. Anyway, MS and I had a pretty deep conversation last night. It mainly was about our relationship so far. We both agree that our personalities clash too much. The simple vocabulary that I share with my friends he finds offensive. My word choice such as dumps, stupid, special, and clearly, he doesn't like too much. He's so sensitive. Maybe too sensitive for me. He's so serious all the time. Indeed, we are attracted to each other, but physical appeal only goes so far. I admire his maturity. He said we should just be friends and get to know each other a little better. I totally agree. I like his way of thinking. I'm not sure what God has in store for us, but I like the way he takes it slow with me. Even though we're not "talking," he still calls me at least once a day. P.S. He makes a good dad! Well, tomorrow is the 10th. Mine and SS's 1st year anniversary if we hadn't broken up. I wonder if I'm going to see him tomorrow, and if he'll say anything to me. I saw him briefly at AY last Friday night. I wonder what he's thinking. But I must admit that I'm happy we say hi and bye to one another. I keep him in my prayers. Lovingly yours, Nicci

December 10, 2001

Dear Journal,

Him: You look nice today.

Me: So, do you.

Him: Yeah! But not as wonderful as You do!

The above is from Sir Michael himself. He's so goofy. Anyhow, he looked so cute tonight. He was wearing khaki-colored polo pants, blue shoes (ha) a black Guess belt, and a beige-colored turtleneck sweater.

Him: So, considering all that was said, you still would be my friend?

December 11, 2001

Dear Journal,

I'm speechless right now. So speechless I can't even pray, only to mention the sweet name of Jesus. Finally, after all these months since SS and I broke up, I finally know...I'm evil. While his roommate and I were in the library, he said a few things that left me speechless. I've come to my own conclusion...I was wrong...

Evilness is I as innocence walks by I sit and I plot, alone, in my own thought. Wondering, how did I get this way still haunts me today. At first, I blamed he who hurt me first, emotionally. Playing foolish games with his heart after a while we split apart. Evilness is I.

Disappointment! I can't finish, my mind is racing. My mother always told me never to hang my head down for I'm too beautiful, but the hurt and pain I have caused deserves a time of mourning, real mourning. If people only knew. I wonder, has God already forgiven me? I'm so wrong. It was all my fault. He broke up with me…I used to think because I wouldn't sleep with him. It's so much deeper than that. I feel so ashamed. I almost started crying in front of Quincy. I'm so dumb. I totally have a Sociology test tomorrow. So many things are going wrong in my life. I'm a pathological liar. I've lied so much to him; he wouldn't believe me from Adam. I said so many evil and harsh things. Disappointment! There is no way a girl like me is going to inherit the Kingdom of God. –Nicci

December 12, 2001

Dear Journal,

Hey, what's up? Nothing much here. I'm about to take this final for my Sociology class. My mind can't seem to shake the thought that QW put in my head last night. Such a time of confusion. But Figurines Danced in my Head…

Opinions, situations, trials, and tribulations. Important figurines danced in my head from sunset to sunset, forever following me to bed.

A quick rebound from depression probably started my confusion. My emotions were like potions, lethal to my relationship that weakened my self-battleship. Split personalities weren't one of my penalties. But figurines danced in my head. My mixed psychology always bothered me. All I can do now is offer an apology. Unforgiven guilt, I kilt, now of yours. But from locked doors. I can't seem to penetrate this thing I have for you called love/hate. But figurines danced in my head. Words to forever go unsaid. You left without a clue from words by who? Maybe it's even true that real beauty isn't I because evilness lurks by. Not at all meant on purpose, but my loving compassion turned to a furnace.

***

At times in college, I would call home to check on everybody, especially my younger brother and sister. This time I had called to thank Dad for sending me $300. I inquired about mom. For the past several months, he would make an excuse for her whereabouts. This time he came clean and told me she was in a half-way house and would be there for a few more months. He said maybe next time we speak, he would three-way us and we could talk. I said okay.

January 2002

Figurines Danced in My Head

How did your love die?

Gone in the twinkling of an eye

I believed it was as great as the sky

For God, had made you my guy

Strangers we are, silently walking by

Questions follow me to bed

Figurines danced in my head.

Indeed, I lacked communication;

I apologize for my confusion

That led to your frustration;

From listening to outside influencing

To our separation

My heart slowly bled

Figurines danced in my head.

This confusion I won't take,

Images of you I cannot shake,

Bottled emotion I cannot break.

Again, I was left alone balling,

Like the moon slowly falling,

Pondering fantasies of you calling,

Words that will ever go unsaid.

Figurines danced in my head.

Love, Nicci

January 15, 2002

Dearest Journal,

I broke myself yesterday. (SS) I saw twice yesterday. The second time I was in the chemistry department. He looked at me and kept walking. I broke ranks, went outside, and said, "Hi, Shawn!" Afterwards, I went back inside. I didn't stay long enough to watch his response. Just in case he wanted to act sideways with me. My heart can't take any more rejection coming from the likes of his evil self. Anyway, that's all I had to say…

Nicci

January 18, 2002

Dearest Journal,

I'm free, I'm finally free! Thank God, I'm finally free. Mine eyes have been opened; I can finally see. Oh, how I give thanks to only He Who has showed great mercy upon thee? Now I am happy again to be me! I thank my Father abundantly who loves me everlastingly. Oh, I'm free! I'm free! I'm free. Freeing Yours, Nicci

January 19, 2002

Right now, I am sitting in the OC church. I enjoyed the Aeolians special music. I'm sitting by myself in this huge church. I say that I'm not lonely, just content. SS is here. Clearly, he despises the very ground that I walk on. Every now and then I'll glance at his direction. I can tell he's by himself as well. He's such a weirdo. Anyway, I'm feeling like I'm changing or going through some inner spiritual revolution. Last night in AY the guest speaker was talking about God (of course), but he was saying that there are four steps to making yourself at one with God. First, the earth and then the ten commandments. Third, the holy place, and four, God himself. I feel like I'm trying to grasp God. No matter how far I try to reach, I pull myself back. I'm my own obstacle. My own emotions are the strong handle that always pulls me back. But You know, I'm almost there! I've changed a great deal since I was younger, and I'm different. My mind is more assertive, and I pray more often. If time ever is on my side, I know that God is right there along with it. Pastor Nixon is telling a closing story. Every time I hear him speak; I can't get into his presentation. Oh, well, at least I feel God's presence in this place. I've always admired the beautiful stained-glass windows; they remind me that God was there then, and He is here now. Oh, silly me, I almost forgot to tell You …Feliz Sabado. Love, Nicci

March 18, 2002

Lately thoughts of you seem to run rampant in my mind. Your beauty is the ability to put my flaws behind. An invisible essence surrounds you called patience. Between you and me, I enjoy your company. From your compelling story telling the silly way you walk. Your presence is appreciated even if we just talk. I admire your understanding manner and forgiving nature.

March 27, 2002

I can't seem to have a lengthy conversation with you without you debating or somehow altering the way I think. I've learned a great deal about you in the past 2 ½ months, and I've noticed more negative things about you than positive. Politely and tactfully I'll try to bring them to your attention, but you'll usually just debate and blow the whole point off as if it means nothing to you. I don't think we spend enough time together. I don't think you're very affectionate either. In our little "relationship," I seem to be making all the sacrifices. What sacrifices have you made? What have you done for me? Besides calling me when you want something?

July 18, 2002

To: You

You're right, I don't have any nerve. Well, at least not in this situation. So, I chickened out! Big deal, nobody's perfect. Communicating is so hard for me that it's unreal. Everybody has their fears and issues. In this case, mine is self-pride and a little fear of rejection. You know,

I'm not sure on what to say or even how to say it. I wish I could have someone else do this for me. What I'm about to say isn't relevant to anything, by the way. I guess I'm stating it just for the record. Do you remember when I told you that I missed you? Well, I did. I regretted it a couple days later because you continued to tease me about it. Personally, I didn't find it humorous in the least. I prefer writing it down because I don't have to look you in the eye or prepare myself for your debating questions and probes. Reluctant to say, I really like you a lot. I guess denying it only makes me more frustrated every day. I hope I have the confidence to even give this letter to you. I was on the phone with Lee Lee like forever last night. I wasn't getting advice from her, but I had to see what she thought about it. She said that I needed to swallow my pride. But some things are so hard to shake sometimes, you know? I've always felt like I'm left at hello; I hate that junk. I enjoy your company. Or because you're the only one who stayed for the summer. You know me so well that at times I get kind of scared. For real, thoughts of you are always in my mind, constantly. Feeling like my feelings aren't deep; they affect nobody but myself. Talking and fronting gets tiring, real fast. Oh, well, I guess we all live, learn, and move on. Right? (As if you can answer me.) Sorry if I keep jumping around in this letter, but you know I must do a quick subject change here and there. I'm going to keep rambling on until I've clearly said everything that I feel like I should say…Brain Freeze… I get so nervous sometimes that one day I'll do something so stupid you'll never talk to me again. Brain Freeze. I'm thinking about ending the letter right here. Like, Sincerely, Nicci. But that would be the ultimate road. For some reason, showing affection is like mad hard because I try to set barriers and maintain at the same time. That doesn't go so well. (I hope you can read my handwriting because I'm not going to read it to you, not because of attitude, but because I'm a hopeless wuss. At least, I'm admitting to it this time.). Aww man, another Brain Freeze. You know how it takes me like 5 hours to say some stuff? Well this letter speeds the process. Like it doesn't take me 5 hours to just write it; that is another story. I hope you don't clown on me about this letter. I find myself missing xx even if I just saw xx. You know I think this letter puts myself out there. This will be the last time for a hot minute. I admire you, even if You don't admire me. I am for real running out of words to say what I think, but you are smart. You can fill them in. All this time, all this paper, all this ink, just to say that I have feelings for you.

***

I remember it like it was yesterday. He and I sat in my 1988 Mercury Sable parked in the lot of a random apartment building. He had asked me earlier in the week if I wanted to smoke with him. I said yes, and here we were as I watched him preparing the joint. I wanted him to think I was cool. I wanted him to like me, and I was tired of him teasing me about being a "good church girl." I wanted to show him that I could get down with him and his friends too. He sparked it, and I got scared. In my mind I was thinking that I am way too strong for this, and this isn't going to feel like anything. He passed it to me, I took a pull, started to cough and pulled again at the joint. I began coughing uncontrollably, and he laughed at me and called me a rookie.

On December 27, 2002 I gave in to his sexual advances. I was about nineteen and in no way ready for it, but I felt like I was slower than other girls according to him; and he told me that I needed to grow up. As I look back on it now, I was in no way ready for the emotional or psychological aspects of sex. But I gave in, wanting to be like the other girls he always compared me to. No matter what I did to try to impress him, I was always referred to as small, little, a rookie, or some other form of smallness. My wanting his acceptance and trying to prove my coolness to him lead me down a rough road full of drama. We will call him B.

CHAPTER THREE

The Crushing

At the end of 2002, I ran out of money for school. I had to leave, and that left me devastated. My friends, classmates, college life, everything. I was ashamed, embarrassed, and humiliated when I had to pack my room up and move into the hood. My peers got to continue their education without me. I was going to have to figure it out on my own. I didn't come from rich, educated parents. I didn't have a trust fund, or even other relatives that could help me out. The loan I was using expired, they changed the qualifications for it, and I needed a good co-signer. My efforts in finding one failed. I told my mom, but she couldn't find one for me either. She told me to come home, and she would find work for me, and I could enroll at the local community college. I said no thanks and took my luck at living on my own. I didn't know a great deal about life then, but I knew that going back home was not going to happen. At 19, I got an apartment with my boyfriend.

***

November 9, 2003

Dearest God,

Well, You know my heart, mind, body, and soul. You were there during my very conception. You made me. Wherever I am, Ye may be also. Father, forgive me of my sins and trespasses that I have done unto You. Forgive me for my fornication, lying, bearing false witnesses, and for not keeping Your precious Sabbath holy. Forgive me for going astray. Lord, please, forgive me for I know not what I'm doing. Be with me, heavenly Father, through my hardships, trials and mistakes. Heal me now, Father, and make me at one with You again. Touch my confused mind and mend my broken heart; rescue me from my emotions and deliver me from mine inequities. Bless my future and make it bright once again. Blow from Your lips freedom and push my grey clouds away. Instill upon me a steadfast life that blossoms the fruit of the Spirit, where others see in me what You have ordained. Lead me like the children of Israel, part my red sea of sadness, depression, hurt and guilt. Rescue and protect me from my fiery relationship like the three Hebrew boys in the furnace. Pour over me a blanket of hope, tranquility, and a sound peace of mind. Deliver me from my situation, Father, for I can't find the strength to do it myself. Grant me the knowledge, power and wisdom to rise from my bed of sin.

***

B broke up with me. And I went a long time without writing in my journal. Our breakup devastated me, and I found myself constantly on my knees begging him to take me back. He told me that I was a black woman, strong, and I need to act that way. He was with other girls, and sometimes he didn't come home at night. Yes, we still lived together, and I was in a bad place. By the end of our relationship, he was shoving me, slapping me and would borrow my phone, car and money. I was an idiot, and I allowed him to run over me. By the beginning of 2004, I got my own place and tried to restart. I was still trying to recover emotionally from B.

***

January 27, 2004

Dear Journal,

Sorry I have not talked to you in a while, but I got plenty of good news. I haven't smoked in 9 days. I cheated Wednesday though because I had a semi-life crisis. You know that job I've been telling you about? Well, I didn't get it. I failed the drug test. The nurse asked, "Marijuana?" I said, "New Year's." She shook her head. I already knew I messed myself up. She escorted me out the building. I felt like I put a scarlet letter on my own chest. I felt so ashamed, like a loser. This happened on Wednesday, my one-week anniversary from smoking. I told my mom and dad first, then my friends. Big Dogg picked me up, and we drove to pick up this old white guy. I'll call him Uncle Doc. He was a Vietnam veteran. I had to put him in check because he made some crack about having sex with me. I quickly let him know it isn't going down like that. To move along, I cheated. You hear me? I cheated! Not only did I buy a pack of smokes, I partook in half a blunt. I instantly felt bad. Guilty. I had lost a spiritual battle. I just knew God was bragging on me in Heaven. Just like He was bragging on Job, years ago. I let him down. I lost a spiritual battle. I didn't hit no more after that. I gave the rest of my smokes away. It just isn't fun no more. My conscious won't let it be. I prayed and asked God for forgiveness. But, you know, a just man falls seven times. To fall seven times, mean that You must have gotten up six times. I knocked my mistakes off me and kept on trucking. Now, let's talk about Saturday night. G2 called asking for some green. I said okay. He said he'd call when he took his cousin back to his house. I said okay. (Keep in mind the last time I saw him was the Saturday before). Not because of me, but because of him. Like always. He called back and said he found another avenue. I said okay and that was the end of our conversation. I was hurt, again. I haven't seen him all week, and now we are about to go on another week. I wanted to call him back and chew him out, but I charged it to the game; because I'm a hot girl and if a man doesn't want to chill with me, that's on him, his loss. Even though it hurt, I turned on 3ABN and forgot about him. I had planned to spend another evening solo, just me and God. Then, guess who called me back? Guess? G2! He had switched up and said he and his son needed some altering done on their trousers. I said okay. He said they'd be at my house in 30 minutes. I said okay, then hung up. I don't believe nothing he say, so, I just say okay to everything. But just in case I cleaned up a little and took a shower because I smelled like a herd of sheep. As soon as I got out the shower and put my clothes on, there was a knock at the door. After dressing, I went to answer it. Him and his son. I felt instantly uncomfortable. I didn't know how to act or what to say. I thought that I would just ignore Jr. As soon as they walked in, Jr. asked, "You want me to remove my shoes?" I said sure. "How well-mannered," I thought. The whole time Jr. was there, he asked me plenty of questions and addressed me with yes ma'am, no ma'am and thank you and no thank you. He was so polite and sweet; I just could not be mean or ignore him. I'd have to have been a monster. I thought to myself: if G2 acted like Jr., we would have done got married by now. He was adorable. Moving right along. Let's discuss Monday. I had been trying to call G2 Sunday, because he is always lying to me. He said we were going to go out Saturday night, but he fell through. Said he was going to call back Sunday evening but didn't. 12:30am Sunday night I tried calling him, no answer. It hurt me again. I felt like I didn't have a boyfriend. He's only good for paying bills, but what about emotional and physical stuff? Very rarely, he is there. I prayed and cried out to God. I told him how lonely I felt and how I am a sheep, him my shepherd, and I need guidance. Guidance so I don't go through the same foolishness that I've twice been through. I got in bed, with 3ABN on, crying out to God. I fell asleep. Monday morning, I felt fresh and new. Things were a lot clearer now. I knew the answer to my problem. It's an answer that I could share with a lot of girls. White, black, Hispanic, Asian, etc. It's awfully simple too. You know how you'll fall for someone and tend to forget certain things? Well, I had to remind myself that I am a beautiful black woman who is independent, I deserve the very best. I am an asset and a priceless investment; I have a lot to offer. And I have a lot to gain for me. I am also a child of God. I'm educated, smart, funny, warm, I can cook, sew, worship my creator, and I use my head. I decided I don't need him. I don't need him. I'd rather be by my own lonesome than be a part of a relationship that my companion is trying to set me up for the

Okie Doke. Monday came and I tried calling him; he hung up. I called again because I wanted to say what I had to say, even if it was on his voice mail. The second time I called, he answered. In a calm, collected voice, without cursing, I told him. Of course, he tried reaching in his bag of many tricks to fool me, but I quickly ignored his tactic and kept to the subject at hand. After saying what I had to say, I hung up the phone. Later, I fixed his son's pants and didn't even bother with his stuff. I dropped his belongings off at his job and continued trucking. He blew up my phone for the rest of the day, but I was on cloud nine and he didn't faze me. Now, Monday night. P got bent and put her newborn on me. So, I stayed up all night with the baby. Now I am going to go to the auction tonight at 7 so I can sell my old Caddy to pay bills; pray for me. Love, Nicci

June 9, 2004

My Treasures Are in Heaven

Last night, I was hungry, and my body a long time infected. No medicine, no money. My car is smoking. I live in a shoe box. My clothes are worn and have holes. My wants forever to go empty; Satan reminds me of this everyday

I remember, my treasures are in Heaven.

I have a sore heart that's still healing I'm skinny and feel nasty. Loneliness is a constant companion; selling blood for money, scavenging to eat. Ssshhh, it's a secret, for I don't want to burden anyone. Maybe I'm not living right. God, do You see me? Satan reminds me of this every day.

I remember, my treasures are in Heaven.

Attending college, sometimes no gas to even get there. I've been arrested and thrown in jail with crackheads and prostitutes for not having any money. My friends and family have burned my emotions time and time again. Satan reminds me of this every day.

I remember, my treasures are in Heaven.

October or December 2004

Dear B,

I'm not sure what words I should use to say what I need to. I haven't been returning your calls for many reasons. Many I'll fail to mention.

But I will bring to your attention a few. I know you're not my real friend. I won't bother with any explanations because I know you wouldn't care to hear. Maintaining any type of relationship with you is unnecessary. I'm positive you know why. Nicci

August 1, 2005

Dear God,

I'm sorry, for I hurt You time and time again. God, I'm so sorry. I deserve this, to be alone. To never live. I deserve this. God, I'm sorry. I'm late to church; I don't go. Cursing, smoking, drinking, I'm on drugs. God, please, even though I deserve it, please don't leave me. Figurines that were dancing in my head, I don't play their music. They stand around all dressed up, waiting for me. "Play our music," they say. "No", I reply, God, B is mean to me. I'm just a disappointment! "There, dance to that!" they look shocked, perplexed, shaking their heads. "Go, turn your back to me!" I continue. Fine! Do it! That's real talk! Your shame is hanging out! Dudes are gone run thru you in the 'Ham. "Mrs. X has a ring to it, what you think?" Look at pretty Nicci. Yella Bone up in the house. Who is that? Her elusive shadow,

'Lonely.' He's clear. B's not. He's Dark. You all have hurt me. Even more, my list is greater. B has hurt Nicci. Stop! Don't be mean to Nicci. "She's just a little girl, a baby." Help me, God! Help me, God! Help me, God. I'm just a little girl. A little girl. Save me, Father.

Perishing Solo

By myself I live, forever and forever I give, by and by friend's use. Take and take, keep taking. Deep inside I'll perish solo.

Loneliness is my best friend, for he'll never leave me. My elusive shadow, Perishing Solo. Followed by my elusive shadow. No children, no love, no one. I'll perish Solo with my elusive shadow.

April 5, 2005

This one goes out to all the dime girls heading to get their riches. Y'all know how we do, showing up in the club with a new hairdo. Pulling up in an automatic Diablo, hating chicks go "whoa!" Door opening two-tone interiors. Step out, the whip twitching it when I walk, goods in bulk.

September 20, 2005

Here we go again.

Gusts of a whirlwind, my nature is repeating its course.

Soon, yelling matches will come and make me hoarse.

Making my feelings all mangled, and the dancing figurines.

Y'all get on my last nerve. Spiderman will not spin a web and get me all tangled up in his trap of lies. It is those butterflies, you are a poacher, always hurting. A snake slithering between cracks and crevices, creeping along past barriers. My head threw my heart a knife and whispered, "But free yourself. Fore it's too late." Under the influence of Mary Jane,

Sipping on Mr. Bud Lite, I think we should just be friends.

Rather chill by my lonesome.

October 14, 2005

Dear Journal,

Wow, it's been a long time. Well, today I just sat around and watched TV, read, slept, and ran off at the mouth on the phone. My heart feels so heavy right now. Millions upon millions of figurines are dancing in my head again. Well here's my list of figurines.

I'm B's plaything, he doesn't love or care about me. I deal with him because I've been doing it for so long. And...no excuse; I wish I were married. I'd never feel alone, and I wouldn't have to be with different men for love and affection. G2 is a liar. He says just like B did that he's going to wife me. But now, I don't believe anything that comes out of a man's mouth. I've slept with him like 5 or 6 times. It just doesn't seem quite right. I don't trust him. Never have, I just can't. I'm going to listen to that voice this time because last time I got mixed up. My job is Satan's playground; it's like a pimping headquarters. I rob, steal and cheat them. I'm caught; I feel ashamed, but I'm kind of glad because I don't feel like I belong there anyway. Liquor, smoke, disrespectful, walking unpleasant. I belong at home after dark.

Why do I hurt so much? And for so long? Every day is a struggle. I need something that will help my loneliness. G2, he's a spoiled rich man. Always talking about how much he loves me. He's supposedly my boyfriend. But I don't understand why he's trying to play me. He is playing me, right? I maybe will see him once per week. But he calls me every day. I didn't answer the phone today because I'm confused. Let's do the Libra thing and weigh it. Good: takes me out, calls every day, he's my friend, asks me how I feel, and tells me how it is. Bad: I don't trust him, I can't picture being married to him, supposedly works a lot, cheated on his last wife, and broke up with current girl to get with me.

His wealth just doesn't impress me. I'd rather marry a trash man who doesn't work all the time, but I can trust him, and he'll spend more time with me. More time with me. More time with me. More time with me. Why do I always think about that? Could it be because I'm so lonely? I don't want my future mate getting tired of me. But I long to be around another body. One that can talk to me, care about me, and take care of me mentally, physically, emotionally and of course spiritually. But I'd give back too! I wouldn't be just a taker. I would take care of him as well.

***

During this time, I felt the spirit of God tugging at my heart. I had let so much build up inside of me, and I was barely hanging on. Even in my drug and party times, I still looked forward to going to church. Seeing everybody dressed up, hearing the choir, listening to the pastor passionately speak of God. It fueled me in a weird way. I knew I needed to head back to God. I just couldn't figure out how.

***

October 15, 2005

Dear Journal,

Well, I made it! I'm in church. I was almost on time for divine worship. I feel good. I've tried Mt. Calvary SDA. I like it a lot better than OU. It's smaller, more personal. I'm undercover, going unnoticed. A beautiful Children's Choir is singing, 'Down by the Riverside.' Sing it, babies!!

I keep thinking about G2! While pulling into Mt. Calvary, I saw xx park in the row in front of me...two girls. They just happened to turn into the church that I chose to go to. I've seen the driver before where I use to work. I believe G2 even brought her up there. I vaguely remember complementing her on her sandy blonde hair color. I believe she is one of his nieces. They look a lot alike. But people say that we look alike. Is that his niece? I wonder what her name is. I don't believe nothing that comes out his mouth. (I feel so beautiful here! The church has a heavenly aura! It's a struggle between the negative and positive when it comes to G2.

October 17, 2005

Dear Journal,

Where should I begin? I got the whole world closing in on me. Well, at least my world is closing in on me. It all started this morning; xx said I couldn't move over there because someone said I have "illegal" animals in my apartment. I already paid my deposit for my cat. And my iguana should not matter because he is a baby and do not bother nobody. My apartment has water damage, and the Community Development came to my house on 09/28; they even said I have mold growth in my cabinetry. Nicci's list of problems: apartment, my job, rumors, G2, friends, smoking, drinking, and cursing. But, praising God in the meantime.

November 3, 2005

Last night was crazy. Since Jim aided me in my move from one apartment to another, plus he has always helped me time and time again, I started to feel differently about him. He never asked for it back, or even for some type of collateral. John wouldn't let me work cause of some stupid scheduling conflict. Anyway, I invited Jim over. We got a movie, a pack of Bud Lites, and I got a sack of some fire from Big Dogg. At first, I felt bad and guilty about it cause if G2 knew, he would be mad. But after chilling with Dancing Jim, I discovered many things. Now, Jim is the opposite of me. He's about 70 or 75, white, widowed and rather wealthy. I used to think of him as just an income source. Now, I value our relationship. I've known him for about 2 years on and off. But I want to mention the difference between him and G2. He is not like G2, he's different. In a much better way. I mean intellectually (setting aside color) I can bounce things off him. To me, meaningful things that make me feel rather positive. I can trust him. Except for him always being touchy feely; I didn't mind, though it irritated me a little. I enjoyed his company so much that I tolerated it. From about 10pm to 2am. He's not negative about me like G2. But I must keep in mind that I've known Jim longer than G2. He's a womanizer, I know he's not the one. But he keeps insisting that he is. I've told him this. Oh Journal, what am I to do? I don't want to get caught up again so please help me God not to get caught up in a web of hurt again. Love, Nicci

November 4, 2005

You won't believe what happened last night! G2 was sleeping, and I was playing a game on his phone. Y's call came in. He was sleep, so I answered the phone! The drama hit the fan! For real! This is how our conversation went:

Me: Hello?

Her: Is G2 there?

Me: He's sleeping; can I have him call you back?

Her: Who's this?

Me: Nicci.

Her: You're his girlfriend?

Me: Yes.

Her: Can I please talk to him? It's important (sounding shaky).

So, I said sure and passed the phone to him. He was coming out of his sleep and she said, "Hello?" She sounded so hurt. "G2? G2?" When he finally woke up, she said something like, "You're cheating on me?

You're sleeping with her?" I was surprised but not shocked. I kicked him out and chewed him up in the process. After he left, my phone started blowing up. He remained calm. For an experienced liar, he faithfully stuck to his lie and tried feeding me some foolishness like, "She's married, she's not important, I haven't cut that in like 5 months!" My logic is like, what is a married woman doing calling him every night. You had sex with a married woman? If she's nobody, why does she keep calling you?

November 5, 2005

Dear Journal,

Right now, I'm at SDA Church to hear my uncle preach. I figured that coming to church will cure my hate for G2. I can't stand him. Our 13-year age difference is really catching up with me. Journal, I can't stand him. Last night he wanted me to meet up with him at the barber shop so we could exchange trucks because mine has brake problems. To make a long story short, he made a stupid comment about my age. In return, I got up, walked out, got in my truck and drove off. This foolish man had the nerve to leave me a voice mail talking about he's outside wanting to switch vehicles, and he wanted his old CDs back. Man, if I wasn't a Christian, I'd tell him where to go and how to get there You Big Liar!

November 10, 2005

Hello, how are you? I'm fine. I went to class today for about an hour. Then I bought about 10 old books. I only paid $3.78 for all of them. What a deal! I worked last night. I gave my number to this guy named Cedrick. He said he was going to take me shopping. Will see. He's just a green mission anyway. I should feel bad because G2 is my "boyfriend," but I don't because I'm not doing anything with him. I just want to go shopping like for real and do some serious damage. Me and G2 are doing okay now. Maybe we will have a future. I thought about him from the time I got off at 2am til about 5:20am before I fell asleep. I was thinking about what he commonly repeats to me, like, all the time.

1. You don't respect me.

2. Why do you always have to curse?

3. Cancerous.

4. Our kids/marriage

5. You'd make a good wife.

Nicci's response:

1. G2, what makes you think I don't respect you? Do I curse too much around you? Should I not do it? Do you wish to have the same respect I give my parents and Gramps? Maybe that was what you are talking about. From early this morning on, I will add some more things to my "don't do around G2" list.

   a. Cursing (I'll try), smoking pot (already exists), giving him TMI, brain freeze

November 11, 2005

Dear Journal,

G2 took P and I out last night. I think P kind of showed herself a little. She kept hounding our poor waiter. G2 tipped him well, so he really didn't care in the end. He irritated me a little during dinner. But those feelings quickly subsided. Journal, I think I'm getting a little bit better. I got some good books to keep my busy bee mind thinking. After dinner, Big Dogg, G2, P and I went to her house to watch "Uncle

Buck" starring John Candy and Macaulay Calkin. Near the end, G2 and I left. I was going to go home solo, but he wanted to tag along. I enjoy his company, but I don't really want to start getting attached to him. I gave in, and he came to my house. He brought a drink for himself (he doesn't like water as much as me!), a deck of cards, fruit and nut mix, and a very big tube of unique lotion. I have lots of lotion in my bathroom. Why did he buy me some? Is my skin ashy? What is he trying to say? How embarrassing that my so-called boyfriend must tell me about paradise gold cocoa butter premium lotion. Sounds nice, huh? I kept all these thoughts to myself and said a plain, "thank you." We played 2-man spades, he taught me a card trick, and I watched him doodle on a piece of paper. I kind of been waiting on it. It feels so interpersonal. Just like MB doodles earlier. G2 is very smart. He's down to earth, kind, compassionate. I've always wondered about rich people and how they are different from commoners. Why did God make them the ones with money and not good people like others? Or I used to wonder why G2. I thought that there must be a reason as to why God gave G2 all that he has. Like Job, or King David. Or even Bill Gates or Donald Trump. I finally have figured out why God gave it to G2; I learned this about a day or so ago. He gave it to him because of his way of thinking and his heart. I used to look down on him for having half of his family living with him. And putting them all up (most of them anyway); his heart is bigger than mine. Especially with P, he is the one that invited her to dinner, not me. The monkey or figurines in my head would try to throw in that G2 might fancy her a little, because he is accursedly promiscuous. But I believe it was because of his empathy. Indeed, he is becoming a piece of work. Rather impressive. I'm glad God chose him to bless. Ironically enough, he still burns me up sometimes. Like asking me at dinner with P if I was planning to breastfeed. What in the world? I'm not too sure if he was trying to crack on my bust size, but I don't look like a cow! I mean, what? I'm a 23-year-old college student working to graduate and get a decent job to support myself. Breastfeeding, G2, is the last thing on my mind! I mean, gosh! Then to come up again from the peanut gallery level, he asked what my ring size is! O my goodness! Can you please reduce speed by like 10 years! Calm and slow down. Shhhhh, G2 is still sleeping. It 2:23am and I'm about to shower. I'm taking my tired self to bed. Love, Nicci

November 12, 2005

Dear Journal,

Happy Sabbath! I didn't go. Last night was crazy. G2 signed a 1998 Toyota Rav4 to me. The bill of sale and everything in my name! That rocked my world! I didn't know what to say. I asked P what I should say to him. She said, "Thank you?" So, that's all I said. I wasn't sure if I should act refined, get excited, act surprised or even be wary of his gift. Wow, it's confusing. I'm not sure what to say. G2 advised me to let P hold my whip. I listened to him and gave her the keys. I got mixed feelings for P sometimes. G2 can break my heart's ice when it comes to P. I feel better about the situation. But as I think about it more, I remember a prayer from about 2-3 weeks ago that I had with God. I know P needed a car because of her new baby and he/she will have doctors' appointments and P can't be walking in the winter to get to a bus. I told God that if I can afford it, when I get a new one, she can floss the Cadillac. It happened; God gave me one. Or was it G2? I'm not sure, but at lease P has transportation now and her soon-to-come baby.

November 16, 2005

Dear Journal,

Hey, how are you? I'm fine. I would call Jim or text him and he wouldn't respond; he always responds. I knew something was wrong. So, I called again when I got back from Nashville. At about 5:30am. While I was asleep, he called me back. He said that he had a double heart attack! I knew it! He assured me that he didn't need any help because he had plenty of family and friends taking care of him. Isn't that something? Then I got a call from G2; his uncle had passed away in the night. So, he went down to be with his family. He left yesterday and will be back Thursday afternoon (tomorrow); a little part of me thinks he's lying to me to spend a couple of days with one of his many lady friends. But I'm going to give him the benefit of the doubt. So, I sent my condolences. You know, I can't even hold water from you! There have been a few things on my mind: Ariel, B, and G2. We will start with G2 since it was the latest. I must admit, I was high as the stars. But G2 called me. Tasha had showed up to his house, and we were talking about it. He had asked me for my advice, and I didn't say much. He recently has come up with a new word to describe me..."

You're so appreciative," he says. "I don't really do a lot for you." Or another occasion, we were talking about the new car he gave me. I don't remember the whole conversation, but he had said something like, "It wasn't like it was expensive." Throughout our many talks he has said how much he has done for V and N (his exes). At first, I use to look at them as lazy bums. But from his little remarks, I started thinking differently. Let me give you a little history before I break my feelings down. I am an independent woman. I don't need anybody. I pay for my own, and I work extremely hard. I handle rent, insurance, phone, nails, toes, hair, utilities, gas and my own food. It's been like this for years, and I don't depend on anyone. Or even expect anything from anyone. I am very proud to say this. From how G2 describes his exes, they are my opposite. He took care of them. That's fine, no hard feelings, but just one. Even the pickup truck that he let me borrow had bad brake problems. His niece had a bigger, shinier rig than me when I saw her. Journal, I'm grateful, but right now, I'm venting. He does do a lot for me, but if I were to quit my job like he wants me to, the money that he does give me occasionally, would NOT! be enough to make me comfortable. Journal, please don't think I'm being ungrateful, but in my head, there is a red flag. Compared to everyone else, G2 gives me the leftovers of everything. There it is, he has even said so himself. So, what will I do about it you ask? Absolutely nothing! For right now, something is better than nothing. Wow, I feel a lot better. Besides, I'm a patient person. In due time, the subject will come up again and depending on my mood, it'll be handled. But, no sweat, cause unlike V and T, I don't need him. But I do enjoy his company. P.S. I knew it b4 he said it. Ssshhhh. Love, Nicci

November 17, 2005

Dear Journal,

I went to class this morning and turned in my essay for Mr. F's class (American Lit.) P helped a whole lot on it. She basically wrote the whole thing. I felt kind of bad about it. But she kept insisting despite my objection. She said that I was too high (cop out) and that it was fun considering that she hadn't been to school in years. While she was busy writing it, I stared at her. With a million and one things going through my mind. I began reminiscing on P and I even thought I have gone a lot out of my way for P; she always restores why I call her my friend. She has made breakfast for me, helped with homework, moving my stuff, giving advice, and always answering the phone. I guess the pot made me feel like extra emotional, and I felt highly impressed to give her my car. Just like G2 gave me. I wanted to bless her like God blessed us. She is 8 ½ months pregnant. It reigned in my mind, whether I should keep and sell it for profit or give it to her and trust God to take care of me. I was in a dead spot. So, I called my wise father. He said a heart was not a thinking organ, it's emotional. "Use your head." If you're going to give it away, give it to someone in the family like your mother or little sister (14 years old). He also said that she might start looking at me like something other than a friend. She might start asking for more and more, beginning to get greedy. He said it would be wiser to sell it and the surplus could be given to her. He said I could even lease it to her. To teach a lesson, like he did me. I'm personally still thinking. I do need a dining table, winter clothes, groceries and rent! Sell it! The scales on xx is neutral as for night now. The whole car thing is still having me leary. Work last night was crazy. But I saw plenty, didn't make too much either. But xx's nephew and brother were in the spot last night. I believe that I have them figured out. Shawn says bad news first! He's a poser that lives with his uncle. He has 2 kids, a small boy and girl that live in Chicago or maybe Ohio. Anyway, sources say he currently lives with his uncle because he is saving for an apartment. He's been saving for over a year! And yes, ladies and gentlemen, it's Alabama! So, you know rent is cheap! So, his "saving" can be translated into freeloading in the 1st degree. Second, he stays loud in the club with his name-brand shoes, pants, shirts and hats. I'm not even going to mention the fur coat! But his profile is stamped with big red letters, Fake Rich! Terry, on the other hand, has a more legit purpose for clubbing. Checks out girls getting drunk and number catching. He is not a want to be for real show boater like his nephew. He has plans of opening an auto body shop. Extremely productive and ambitious; his profile can be cool! Thank you, Love, Nicci

November 22, 2005

Hey Journal,

I was just cleaning up the kitchen and I came across this receipt. I decided to save it as a keepsake. Since I do not get cards and letters from him, I will act like this is a red hot, steaming love letter. With Love, Nicci

November 27, 2005

Dear Journal,

Our first movie was fun! G2 and I saw harry Potter 4! I was shocked he wanted to tag along. Not too much to say. My parents are going to be here at 8am tomorrow morning. I'm feeling nervous, anxious, excited, relieved, and everything in between all at once. I haven't lived around my parents in 6 years. I'm a changed person now. I've matured, and I have become an individual. I'm a little scared that something bad is going to happen. I constantly hear G2 talking about this shrink named Richard. He practically begs me to talk with him. My argument is always the usual, "I'm not crazy!" I've never been through anything in my past. There is no reason for me to act the way I do; I'm just like this!" If G2 only knew I am a lying sack of rotten potatoes. Straight and flat out lying through my teeth! Man, I know that talking to Richard the shrink would probably be the best thing for me. But I couldn't possibly let G2 know. Because it would really bring down my face value! I'd never talk to Richard the shrink. But I do fantasize about it sometimes. I imagine finally telling someone about me–Nicci. The Nicci nobody knows. Opening to a perfect stranger. Easier said than done. I'd tell him about my early childhood. And how close to perfect it was. Then in the next session I'd tell him how my emotional roller coaster took me for a long ride from about 13 to 17. I almost died, nearly killed myself about 5 or 6 times. How life was for me, what my thoughts were, I would tell him everything! In our next session I'd bring out the Goliath coaster! And smack him with that! Poor Richard the Shrink, he'd be seeing a shrink after listening to me! Ha Ha Keep ya chin up, Love, Nicci

December 1, 2005

Dear Journal,

The beginning of my day and last night was quite rocky, I must admit. My family came in this morning. It didn't positively sink in until the second time I saw them today. Now, I am comfortable. When I took my father and mother to my apartment, they acted like it was the Buckingham Palace! They just praised and praised me. Dad started praying and rejoicing to God; he said he was proud of me. After tonight, it has sunk in–God's many, many blessings He has bestowed unto me. From my new apartment to my new coat, not beginning on my new car, dining room set, and groceries. Forget about the new shoes and clothes, He has been so good! Glory be to my maker. I've come so, so, so, so, so far. I used to sell plasma (blood plasma) 2 years ago to pay bills, filing unemployment, using food banks, and welfare. He's been too good. Praise God. I want for nothing, not even a pair of socks. Because he's got my back, my entire back. Thank You, Jesus. He's brought me so far! Today, this beautiful and blessed morning hour of 2:30am, this one's for You! Thank You, Jesus. Love, Nicci

December 1, 2005

Dear Journal,

Good afternoon! I skipped class this morning (it's the end of the semester and I already have an A). Anyway, G2 is coming back in town tomorrow afternoon. He's weird. I wonder about him. Is he for real? Does he really love me? What? Me? Why? Why does he seemingly think so highly of me? My parents, grandparents, sister, brother, friends, co-workers, and even my enemies think highly of me. Why God, why? I'm a liar made from dirt. I'm shady and two-faced. Why? I am so not perfect. I smoke nasty cigars and pot is my constant prescription. I drink and haven't been to church in like 3 weeks. Why God? Why do You do for me? Why? My very best is as filthy rags. Why? Could it be slightly possible that G2 really, really could love me? Why? I got G2's profile:

1. He's not easy to understand.

2. He appears gentle, kind, sympathetic, and a patient listener.

3. You want desperately to be loved and approved of, but resent needing approval so badly.

4. When you get what you need, you give in return.

5. Those who make you feel secure command your undying loyalty.

6. When you really care for someone, there is nothing anyone can say about them that will make the least bit of difference.

7. G2 has a real blind spot when it comes to seeing a failing in those he loves (his family).

8. Beneath his tough exterior, he is a somewhat sentimental softie who will make any sacrifice for someone in need.

9. He is possessive: anyone who becomes part of his life will never be entirely free.

10. You stay in touch with friends, ex-lovers, former wife, business associates, and people You knew as children.

…to be continued. P.S. Praise God. Love, Nicci

December 3, 2005

Dear Journal,

Happy Sabbath! Revelation 22:1-? Whoa, I made it! After a long and hard 3 weeks. G2 is okay; we chilled last night. I was cooking Sabbath dinner last night, and he came through with some Steak Out. After cooking (I kind of burned a patty or two. G2 makes me nervous, and when he's around, sometimes I forget about the situations at hand). I took a shower and G2 told me to wake him when I got out because we were going to catch a movie. When I finished, I went to wake G2 up.

And guess what? Yes, he played me. By refusing to wake up. I just charged it to the game and went to sleep myself. Morning came at about 9:30am. I like sleeping next to him. Anyway, he got on his famous phone and began running off at the mouth. He finished his conversation, gave me a hug, and left. He didn't go to church with me, but that's not a surprise because he has never gone to church with me. Oh well, I'll just charge that to the game also. But it does upset me. There is no way on God's green and blue earth that I'd possibly marry a man that can't take me to church. All in all, I'm in church now. Thank You, Jesus. Love, Nicci

CHAPTER FOUR

Walkabout

During this time, I was working at a local bar. I started with waiting tables, then I was promoted to actual bar tending. The money I made there was pretty good. It supplied my drug and alcohol habit, and it also allowed me to provide for myself. The environment was grimy, and the men that I used I would usually meet at work. Trap music, selling sex, gambling, and drug deals happened here during the operating hours. This job was my lifeline into foolishness, and it fueled my lusts.

****

December 4, 2005

Dear Journal,

Last night was crazy, and this morning not better. I got to work at about 7 pm. About 2 hours later, IA shows up everything was cool. I had to go into my boss's office (JL) to get some pool balls. All present? Me, IA, Dee and J himself. He began to tease, mock, and belittle me sarcastically. My feelings and heart sunk. Soon IA joined Dee and co-signed with laughter. I was mortified, humiliated, and embarrassed. All throughout elementary, middle school, and halfway through high school, I was picked on and a laughingstock. And once more, after an 8-year break, I was back in school dealing with the same old immaturity. Tension between us escalated, and soon she was looking for a brawl (blocking my way, giving me crazy looks, invading my space). I don't want my grill busted up. I don't even want to lose 1 strand from my new weave. Nope! Forget all of it. This job isn't worth it. I grabbed my purse (tried talking to John about it but he laughed it off) and left. Andrew called me. He told me to call and talk to John; I said I would. But I'll put it off. Didn't tell Andrew that. I got kite high, toasted, and fell asleep. Zzzzzzz 1 sheep, 2 sheep, 3 sheep, 4 sheep, 5 sheep, 6 sheep, 7 sheep, 8 sheep, 9 sheep, 10 sheep, 11 sheep. 11am comes. I wake and grab some vanilla soymilk and mini wheats (frosted). Went to my phone, and Punch had called me. I returned the message. To make a long-drawn-out conversation short, here it is in a nutshell: She saw G2 with his cross-eyed, ugly, bad bodied, bright faced, bugaboo, ex-girlfriend. HERE WE GO AGAIN WITH HIS LYING, DOUBLE-FACED DISAPPOINTMENT! But you know what? It's all good. I'm going to roll with his behavior. I'm going to sound cheery when he calls me. Hey, sir! or Sup, baby? Yup, and casually inquire about what he did last night. If he breaks clean, or if he tries to lie, it will be the same reaction. Lord, have mercy, I haven't got the foggiest idea right now. Help me, Father. I don't want to use Punch's advice. God, give me Yours. I want Your guidance. Please, help me. I'm on a rowboat in the ocean of life on earth. Huge waves and bad weather are trying to sink my wee rowboat. I'm hanging on, God! My boat is rocking. You said You would not give me more than I could handle, You have a plan for me, and You love me. So, God, I'm not asking for You to rescue me. I am asking You to make my grasp of my hands tighter. In the meantime, Praise God. Love, Nicci 2:30pm

December 7, 2005

Dear Journal,

Well, you already know what time it is in my life. Not going so well. I'm still a little perplexed about G2. He called me like 5 times today. I was asleep; he left me a couple messages. I checked them. But didn't bother calling him back. I just don't feel like being bothered with him or his coat of much foolishness. I was starting to like him. How in the world is he going to come to my apartment with scratches on his back? And going to have the nerve to tell me he had an itchy rash. Is it just me or do I have an invisible tattoo on my forehead that reads, "Dumb, Stupid, Gullible?" Maybe I just don't see it, but G2 sure does. I guess I'm back at square one again. I got about $200 in the bank, a $157 phone bill and I just quit my dead-end bar tending job. My dad is going to give me his computer system tomorrow til they move in their own place. My old school friend, Carletta, was trying to put me on to doing some internet business. I'm going to try it. But in the meantime, I'm going to hit up some nursing homes for a CNA position. G2 is crazy! But wish me luck with my CNA job and internet business. Praise God. Love, Nicci

December 10, 2005

Dear Journal,

> *"¹Then Job answered and said, ²How long will ye vex my soul, and break me in pieces with words? ³These ten times have ye reproached me: ye are not ashamed that ye make yourselves strange to me. ⁴And be it indeed that I have erred, mine error remaineth with myself. ⁵If indeed ye will magnify yourselves against me and plead against me my reproach."*
>
> —Job 19:1-5 KJV

It is I, Lord, a common man. Drenched in sin and iniquity. Some men are born to be rich and dressed in fine garments. Some men are born to be poor. Dressed in hand-me-downs. They shop at secondhand stores, on welfare, and stand in food bank lines. Their fathers sometimes can't afford to give them lunch money. Or even to make a lunch to send them to school with. Two cups of oatmeal, five children. What would a rich father do? I'd rather live poorly in a shack with God than in a mansion without Him. Am I an underachiever? Dear God, I'm worthless, nothing, an aimless underachiever. Desperately wicked. God, heal me. Touch me. Touch me, Father, and make me a Christian, an upright woman of God. Please help me to stop smoking, drinking, cursing, being slothful, fornicating, bearing false witness. Save me, God, before it's too late! Lord, give me a clean heart for Christmas. Love, Nicci XOXOXOX

December 11, 2005

Dear Journal,

Last night was crazy! Earlier this week B called. He asked if I had a shell. I told him to hold on so I could check. I came back to the phone and told him that I didn't have one. He said that he didn't have enough time to stop and get one and then smoke with me because he had plans later. I was upset a little, but I was like, "That's fine!" and the conversation ended after I accused him of trying to play control games. About 3 minutes later, he texts me, "Be there in 15 minutes." He came over, twisted it up, and as we were chiefing, he began talking noise. I was telling him about G2. Even when I'm mad at him, I always bring him up to B. I told B that he is not respecting my relationship with G2...because of him constantly calling me and wanting to spend the night. I also told him that G2 is uncomfortable with it anyway. Then, B stiffed himself up and said, "He needs to be respecting me! If it wasn't for me passing you along, he wouldn't have you!" Journal, I hit the roof. But I kept my cool. I stood up and said, "Well, it is getting late, and I'm about to go to bed; and since I'm a pass along..." He froze and refused to budge. "Oh," I added, "have a happy holiday and good life." He tried to interrupt with, "Just say good night." He tried desperately to apologize. But I wouldn't hear it. I began turning off the lights, and I opened the door. Slow and reluctantly, he headed to the exit. To me, he just wasn't moving fast enough. So, I put my hand on his back and gave him a firm but gentle push. He switched up and said, "Get your hands off me. I can leave on my own." Not a moment went by when I slammed the door behind hm. Two seconds later, he knocked on the door. Talking about he left his keys, and I snapped back and told him he ain't got no keys in here. So, he left. I smoked and fell asleep. Anyway, back to last night. Since G2 was playing the "I'm not going to answer the phone" game, I called my friend Jonny; Punch called her dude M to meet us. I picked up E and some Mary Jane on the way. E and I smoked on the way. We arrived at the club and stood around for a few minutes. Jonny came up and chatted with me. Then, he started a conversation with Punch. Jerk Face comes out of nowhere and begins standing next to me (B). I was mad. Just furious. I was so high. I kept thinking about how much I used to love him and how I used to long just to be in his presence. Even after he broke up with me, he wouldn't let me go. In the meantime, he treated me bad. Belittling me, smacking me, disrespecting me. When G2 and I made it official, I thought I was through with B then. Now, after what he said a couple days ago, I can't stand him. I look at him so differently now. Last night, I was shining like a twinkling star in the sky. And this sorry man was trying to rain on my parade! My girls and I relocated. Guess what? He and his friends followed us. And started lingering in my view. He also tried to pick a fight with Jonny. B kind of ruined my night. We left, I dropped my girls off, went home, smoked, and fell asleep. Love, Nicci XOXOXOX

December 17, 2005

Dear Journal,

Happy Sabbath! I'm at my grandma's church. I stood up my home team last night for Bible study. I smoked, cleaned the house, showered, and waited for G2. He said he'd be there at about 9:30

pm...but 9:30 turned to 10:30 and 10:30 turned to 11:30. After a while, midnight came, and I gave him a courtesy call. He didn't answer. I called about 3 times. He finally called me back at about 12:03 am. He sounded half sleep. He gave me the same excuse he gave me last Saturday night and the days before that. He's falling asleep 4 times on me in the past 2 weeks. His little game is getting just about as old as him. I think the age difference is catching up with me. Especially when he said that he wanted to continue what we were doing Thursday night (wink wink). So anyway, he made me a promise and, like a gullible girl, that's what I was expecting. Got my hopes all up and then just crashed them come midnight. I was so pissed, just fit to be tied, Journal! I confirmed what I was hearing from him by asking, "So, let me get this right, you fell asleep, again?" "Yeah," he replied. Oh, mercy Journal, in response to his action. Click! I hung up the phone. He called back, so I turned it off. I did it because I could really care less about his reasons. I checked the two messages he left. He said I was being selfish. I don't really care, he irritates me.

December 20, 2005

Dear Journal,

Lots and lots to say for You today. Saturday night wasn't too fancy. There is something about G2. Something always remains a mystery. Journal, to be honest, I don't care to find out the mystery. It's a real negative vibe that I catch occasionally from him. Saturday was a decision to cut him from my life for 7 days – and pray. Well, I prayed. He only called once on Saturday about 5. So, it's not too hard. Tomorrow will be 5 days. I got my report card today! 3.0 (Academic Achievement) praise God! Speaking of God, I got something real heavy I got to holla at Him about, so excuse me, Journal, while I sent a desperate prayer to the heavens. Dear God, thank You. Forgive me of my many sins and transgressions against You. Forgive me, God, for not demonstrating a life that reflects only You. Forgive me for going astray. Thank You for all that You have blessed me with. My new car, tv, computer, apartment, food, clothes, shoes, and my health and the health of my beloved friends and family. Be with my brother in Baghdad. Encompass your soldier angels around him and protect him, God, when no one else can. Bless him. Heal this sin-sick world, Father; it disgusts me. Grant me faith, God, faith in You. I am worried.

Ease my mind. You have brought me way too far to leave me. Bless my household, Lord. Please, help me to get the CNA job. Help me to sell my car. I recently quit my job. I have faith and trust in You, God, to be my provider, protector, guide, and relationship advisor. Bless me, Father. Ease my mind. Joy, God, is what I want to feel. A soft and contrite heart. Victory, glorious victory over cursing, smoking, drinking, lying, and my fornications. If G2 isn't the one for me, God, remove him straight up out of my life! You handle it, Father, not me. Part me and my sins as the east is from the west. Thank You, Jesus, for your undying, everlasting mercy and kindness. Love, your earthly child, Nicci XOXOXOX…. Continued….

Dearest Journal,

I'm confused. I don't know why or even how it started. I just know that it's been there for a while. I'm depressed; it's a struggle just to leave the house. I'm so worried about getting this new job. And bills are quite high. I feel like I'm going to be alone forever. Am I ever going to find a guy that is not a full of drama like G2? B? Silver Back? Mr. Wallace? Huh? I feel lonely again. Even with my home team living here now. But I'd rather be alone with contentment than with someone who belittles me, hits me, lies to me, stands me up, and plays those mind games. Send me someone right! Good night, God bless, Nicci XOXOXOX

December 24, 2005

St. Luke 1:9-26 – Happy Sabbath

Dear Journal,

Luke 1:9-26 A Christmas story. Lots to say today. I finally got G2 figured out. Remember when I told you about him having something mysterious? I also vaguely remember asking you if he really, really loved me. I've found the answer to my question. Deep, deep, down inside, I knew it. He's my dough boy. A sugar daddy. It's not a relationship meant to be interpersonal. It's like a business affair. He's not as serious as he sounds. He'd rather just pay me to be in his life. That's it. I'm a paid friend or escort, if that's what you want to call it. It's like having a leisurely job. Or even being a slight call girl. That's the way he acts. It took a while for me to get the point or his object of our game. And, if I didn't know, I know now. My little sister spent the night with me last night. It was the first night in a while (a long time) that I didn't fall asleep high. It took me a good minute to drift off. Many things were in my head. My eyes started leaking. I thought about the love story my sister and I watched. It made me sad. Will I ever find true love like Alley from the movie? Will I, ever? I felt bad, bad. I don't know why. Why am I lying to myself? I know why, I felt bad. It wasn't necessarily a bad feeling; it was a lonely feeling. But I know my day is coming real soon. Love, Nicci XOXOXOX

December 27, 2005

Dear Journal,

It was this very day in 2002 when I lost my virginity. Journal, Journal, Journal. Last night. So G2 finally called at about 9:20 pm last night. He kept saying how he wanted to sleep with me! I told him that all that wasn't about to go down because I've changed, and premarital sex was a branch I had quit swinging on. He asked if I was serious, I said I was. He said in a roundabout way, "That's fine, but I can't live without sex cause I'm a man; and that's something I just can't let go. But I'm just going to let you know I will be having sex tonight. So how are you going to react if we are out somewhere and my buddy approaches me or you about it?" My heart didn't sink like another girlfriend trying to take life spiritually and hoping that her boyfriend would come along. I expected this from him. So, I said it was fine. Then I asked about who he had in mind. He said he hadn't thought about it yet. So, I had to suggest Y, a woman, married, with a 5-year-old kid, a 30-ish girl that looked something like a 'bugga-bear'. He said she was a possibility. So, I told him to have a good night. He said he'd be having sex Tuesday night, so he'd call me on Wednesday. I inquired about Thursday because I was going to be busy Wednesday. We said goodnight. Click. Love, Nicci God bless.

January 1, 2006

Dear Journal,

Wow! I got to lot to say this afternoon. I'm going to start with Tuesday night. G2 and I had…well, I had felt like talking to him honestly, and he was being cold, smart and rude. No matter what I would say, his response was sarcasm. I hung up on him twice but would then call him back. Each time I'd call, he gave me a difficult response. When I had talked with him earlier, he said he was going to come over at about 6:30 pm. I had just gotten home and hauled groceries (that I had gotten from my grandma's food bank) up 3 flights of stairs. My phone was in my purse, and I had missed his call. When I finished putting groceries away, I saw that he had called. So, I called him back. When I did, his infamous attitude started. He said he was halfway home already, and he was going home to go to sleep. I wanted to see him. He kept being mean to me. The last time I hung up on him, I said to myself, "Ugh!" But I knew something was awkward, so I decided to do the unthinkable…drive to his house. I did; it was about 30 minutes away. As soon as I pulled into the driveway, I noticed a light cut out. It hurts to even write about this. I left the car running. And kept Mike Jones playing on the stereo. I rang the doorbell and knocked. No answer. I went to the side door. Rang the doorbell and knocked. No answer. I began tapping on the windows and calling his house and cell numbers. He wouldn't answer. In the driveway, I noticed his newest truck, his classic truck, and another car that didn't look familiar. I was hurt. The X car had 2 car seats in the back. I knew it was a female's car. She was there. I don't know who. I felt hurt again. He could have told me anything, but he chickened out and refused to open the door. But his garage was open. Revenge crept in and anger swarmed around me. A monster had started growling. Not fast, not slow, just medium. I was about to leave. The monster stopped me. Told me to back up and get out of the car. I did. Told me to go into the garage and grab something that could break glass. I did and found a shovel. As soon as I picked up the shovel, the voice eased. I was going to knock and call one more time. I did. Calmly, the monster told me to put down my phone, keys and lighter. I did. It took over my body. I picked up the shovel and swung good and hard at the window…those stormproof southern windows didn't break! The monster quickly put his tail between his legs and disappeared just as soon as he arrived. Stupid loneliness, depression and remorse replaced him. I hung my head, dropped the shovel, collected my things, got in my car and left. Called him once more. No answer. Suddenly the monster came back and said, "A gun can break the window." There it is, I thought. Then, guess who decided to call? G2! His crusty and trifling self! He throws me something like he is halfway to Nashville, and I flip a toss of a threat.

Click! He calls back. It was too late for reasoning by then; I had checked out. I was in route to Big Dogg's house for a Glock! P calls! Friendly like and rather cheerful, but suspiciously asks what I'm doing on the sly. Playing along to her little game, I politely rushed her off the phone. 3 minutes to Big Dogg's, my feelings change AGAIN! But more rationally. In my mind of much matter, I found a garbage bag and put the rational feelings in it, tied it up real tight, so revenge would win the stupid victory. I put the sealed bag in the glove compartment. And knocked on the door. He answered, invited me in, and I told him about what happened. His wise words reminded me of my treasure in the glove compartment. Their voices were getting stronger. Soon I could hear them coming unglued. Out of the car and through Big Dogg's door. He doesn't notice, but I do. Smack! Right upside my head, they stick like feathers to tar. They win. My feelings change AGAIN! After finding the real answer, I make an excuse to assure Big Dogg that I don't feel crazy anymore and I'm going home. I went home, all while G2's crusty behind is still calling like every 5 minutes. (I forgot to tell you that the voice messages he left on my phone stated that he was home, saw me on his security tapes and I was crazy!) After arriving home, I turned off my phone, got high as the stars and sought for a medicine to help my pain. Didn't find none, but my thoughts came up with a historic drug. Depression, ½ cup. Tune out the world, 2 cups. Turn off my phone for 1 week, ½ cup. Loneliness, 2 ½ cups. Reclusive, 1 tbsp. Rejection, 1 tbsp. Never again, 1 cup. Yup, the recipe that I usually take. Gets me all depressed. Take a few sleeping pills and off to "pass the reality-out land." I awoke at 9:30 to my parents banging on the door for a copy of the keys to the Cadillac for a possible buyer – end of that story.

Everything was turned on Wednesday; I was low key, but I got a little something on Thursday. Since G2 kept calling all day Wednesday, I decided to call him up at about 2 pm. Thursday for some shopping money. He said okay and told me where to meet him. I got dressed and put my game face on. Here is our conversation in a nutshell. He asked if I would leave my key under the mat so we could talk. He said he'd call when he got off work. I said okay, and he gave me $600. After parting, I drove my mom somewhere and went home. Got high and laid on the bed. G2 starts calling. Ask me if I answered? I heard his footsteps coming up the stairs. Then, I heard him knocking on the windows and doors. More calls. Ask me if I answer? I started chuckling and giggling to myself as I heard him. I just had to get him back for what he did to me Tuesday night. As Mike Jones says: "I'm going to stall that dude the way he stalled me! Dude, I'm going to dog you the way you dogged me!" P.S. Happy New Year!

It has been since last March or February of last year when I first went to G2's house. RM was with me. The day had started out as the usual. It was on a Sunday. Cold. R and I use to hang out a lot and our activities were always planned by me. At the time, I had lots of menfolk that I would get things from. Gift cards, money, weed, company, anything. Usually, I would have these guys pay for R and me to go places: movies, dinner, trips, shopping. Things like that. I was a pimp, player. G2 was the newest mission. At the time, G2 was called to entertain me and R since from the first I had met him; he practically broke his neck to be in my face. R and I took the Cadillac. We followed him out to his house. We were bored and had nothing else to do. He drove a Cadillac Escalade. I think it was white. I'm not sure what I expected him to have lived like. It was a 30-minute drive. We passed trailers, small businesses, houses, fields, and woods. Into a small residential community. The road we were on started with double-wide trailer type houses, then we began seeing medium sized, nice houses. A little further and we're entering a long-as-the-Yukon driveway with a humongous red brick house and a smaller, similar building resting at its side. I must admit, I was shocked. R's jaw dropped. My thoughts about him changed, and I felt uncomfortable. I wanted to leave but stayed. What excuse could I have possibly used? The house sits on plenty of land, and I noticed its dark color. It seemed creepy. Cold. He took us four-wheeling. It was so cold outside that I just chilled! Ha Ha (literally). Afterwards he invited us into the house. After a tour, we watched a movie. I'm not sure of how I should put in writing my feelings about him. I thought that he was way over my head, and intimidation got hold of me. I felt so small, peasant-like. I realized that he and I were like Jordache to Chanel. It seemed untouchable. His house was the biggest that I've been in since, I don't know. The ceilings were like 20 feet high as the walls echoed our voices. It was furnished with fancy-type furniture and a state-of-the-art security system. It felt impersonal, vacant, empty, mysterious and cold–even lonely. I didn't like it. Maybe that is why I hardly went out there. I am water and he is vinegar; we just cannot mix. I do not know why; I did not belong there. Love, Nicci XOXOXOX

January 2, 2006

Dear Journal,

Today was weird. Did my grandma's and sister's hair. G2 was his usual lollygagging self. He came through on the late night. We talked, then he left at about 2am. Cleaned Tklingits cage and fed/watered her. Love, Nicci

January 12th, 2006

I know what you are. Who you are. What you are about. I can spell you, L.O.V.E. You are not to be trusted, just used. Sad to say, you can just pay. Yes, I plan to marry. Yes, I want a child maybe or even 2. A boy or girl. I have big plans for my uncreated children. I want them to have a different foundation from what I had. Minus the let downs (and you know what I mean). I want them to be their fathers' first children…to be the center of his attention. I want them to have and come from a good pedigree, if you may, of morals. A man that will be there every day when they wake and sleep. Like my beloved father (earthly), I want him to be physically attractive with good hair. A simple 8 to 4 or 9 to 5. Regular, middle class. Spiritual. A Seventh Day Adventist maybe. Smart with an education. Ya, no babies' momma stuff either. I can't stand that. Why should I have to socialize with his kids (2)? Why? They are another woman's offspring. Not mine.

January 14, 2006

Dear Journal,

Happy Sabbath. I'm here at the xx. I haven't been here in a long, long time. I must admit, I had a blessed week. XX called yesterday morning; he said that I basically got the job. I was relieved, but a little confused cause for me to take it, I'll have to drop my 2 evening classes. But, after discussing it with my board of counselors (the different opinions in my head), I'm going to do what I must do and drop the classes.

January 20, 2006

Dear Journal,

A lot to say today. I stopped smoking Tuesday late afternoon. I stopped smoking everything! Cigars and Mary Jane. I had been smoking every day for months. Withdraws are horrible. I'm getting there. God has been knocking at my heart for a while. Tuesday night I went to a smoker's clinic, hosted by xx. He spoke to me. His words touched my inner soul, and it pushed me to look at the one in the mirror. I saw her, clear as day…she needed a change! Smoking is such a nasty, dirty, gross habit. I can't wait til I'm free of its reigns. Oh Journal, God is so good. I'm blessed, too blessed to be stressed.

Dear God,

Don't stop

Pulling at my heart

Not to let me part

I feel You in my bones

Dancing in my mind

Oh, You're so kind

Don't stop

Being my shepherd

Saving me from going astray

Staying with me every day

Waking me every morning

Comforting me, during mourning

Don't stop

I'm so wicked, dirty and wrong

My best are as filthy rags

Burdens are heavy bags

Thank You, Who? You!!

Don't stop

Love, Nicci XOXOXOX

February 9th, 2005

Dear Journal,

Help me, Father, for I am weak and heavy laden. My mind is fragile and my body a puppet, a part of a scheme. Jesus, help me, aid me in my subconscious and replace my backbone made of jelly. Make me like a diamond. All clean and polished. My sins and transgressions swallow me and drown me with confusion. Make me strong. Be my weakness and transfer it into strength. Help me, Father God, for I can't help myself. When man has forsaken me, be my companion. Oh, Lord, thou are good unto me. Thou have blessed me with many privileges. Thank You, Father, for the bed that I sleep in and the pillow that caresses my head at night. The food that keeps me nourished and the clothes upon my back. The freedom I have and the air I breathe. The water I drink. Thank You, Jesus! Praise God. Nicci, XOXOXOX

February 18, 2006

Dear Journal,

Happy Sabbath! Wow, I haven't talked to you in a while. But I got lots to say. I'll start with this past weekend. G2 was on the ball, and we were doing ok. We had a heart-to-heart Thursday. I asked him if he has ever cheated on me. After beating around the bush, he admitted to 4 times. With Y and V., I could not get mad cause I slept with B twice since we got together. I was a little hurt, but quickly dismissed it. He justified it by saying I made him cheat. Whatever, I thought. Even though, I must admit that I liked him. All he had to do was call. He promised to take me to xx because an old classmate of his had passed away. Well, he took me, and I had a great time. We spent 2 whole days together. He brought me a cute outfit from the mall in xx. His cousin was there, and she got an outfit too. I had gotten my hair done a couple of days before, and we had just left his Auntie's birthday's party. We were all dressed up walking around the mall, in and out of stores. Later we went back to the hotel, slept, woke up and went to Tee's night club. Oh, it was a blast. For the first time, I felt that we could just be happy together. Weird, huh? After dropping his cousins back off at home, we went back to the hotel. (We got something to eat at the corner store because nothing else was open.) The next morning, we went to get lunch, then proceeded back to xx. It was a 2 ½ almost 3-hour drive. He wants me to have a baby with him. He's been mentioning it for months now. I'm just not ready. We were in a little honeymoon stage, but I've got lots to do before I settle down. I need to graduate, get a good job, own a small piece of the world, and build a house on it. And, I'm not so sure if it's going to be with him. He mentioned the baby thing like 4 or 5 times. After a while, I just started ignoring him. All this was last Sunday. I didn't see him Monday, but he called a couple times. Tuesday, Valentine's Day. Oh, the National Love Day. One time a year, lovers old and young celebrate romance with flowers, chocolate, gifts, and candlelit rooms. Sweet nothings are whispered. A true day for G2 and me. I woke up and out of all the Valentine's Days I've had, (which all sucked) this one was going down in history books. My plan was to buy red candles, red streamers, and red balloons to decorate the house with. I planned to make him dinner–Nicci style. I was going to dress up nice for him. I wanted to get my hair done too! My dad and baby brother came over. I stepped outside to call G2. He beat me to the punch and said, "Happy Valentine's Day!" I returned the token and asked him what he wanted to do for Valentine's Day. He said he didn't know. And I asked him what he wanted to eat because I was going to cook for him. He said no and said he was going to take me out when we get to Nashville. I was on cloud number nine. Good, I don't have to cook. He said he was going to be over at 4 pm. It was already 1:30, so my dad helped me pick out this gorgeous dress. I had brought it at a secondhand shop for like $3.95. It was bad as get all out! Anyway, I got my hair done, came back to the house and he came over. He gave me a cute V-Day card and brought me a suede comforter set, along with $200. I showered and sat in the living room with him. His phone kept ringing, he kept answering. I was happy. He gave a light excuse to leave but promised to come back when he was done. Well, Journal, you already know what happened. He played me, again. No Valentines, no dinner, no Nashville. I wasn't surprised, but I was hurt. Bet you he was with Y.

Last night, AF took me to xx. I had a ball. Getting drunk with rich white folks in a white folk's spot, it was fun! Leaving, AF got stopped by the police. It was alright, they let him go if I drove. We (me, him, and his 2 friends) went to IHOP and ate; he invited me back to his place and I said okay, and off we went. He lives in a nice apartment out in Madison. He claimed he's selling his 5,700 sq. ft. home. Anyway, his pad was an amazingly comfortable one. He lights the electric fireplace, candles, and turns on the cable box to some show that made it apparent what he was after. Journal, I had him take me home, and that was it. Til next time. Love, Nicci XOXOXO

February 21, 2006

Dear Journal,

I don't have too much to say today. G2 called yesterday afternoon. He wanted to see me at 7 pm. He called at 6 pm wanting to come over, so

I tried to stall him. In the background, he (G2) heard Big Dogg's voice. He flipped out said, "You cheater" and hung up. I tried desperately to call his cell and his job, but he answered once and told me to never ever call him again and he wouldn't ever call me. I guess he thought Big Dogg and I are bed buddies. But we're not. If we were, I'd tell you about it. I tried calling him 3 or 4 times afterwards, but to no avail. I gave up, got high, and went to sleep. All while I got high, my dearest friend P kept texting me little message with spiritual innuendos. I ignored them and proceeded to fall asleep. It was probably around 7 pm. For some reason, I awoke at like 3:30 am. I checked my voicemail. G2 left me a nicely detailed message ending our relationship because he and his ex-girlfriend, N, had a long talk and she is what he considers "real." They were together for like 4 years. I was just a rebound. I knew he didn't love me. I just knew it. Earlier yesterday I sold some green to E; she came by the house in B's car. His new girlfriend was with her.

I know that one of these days God will hand pick someone for me. Someone that will love me for me and won't switch up like the rest of them. All in all, yesterday was a tough day. G2 really hurt my feelings.

I can't say that I didn't see it coming. Lord, protect me from the evil ones' plans. He's out to destroy me. Please remain by my side, Lord. I know I'm not right, God, but have mercy upon my wretched soul and forgive my sins, transgressions, and iniquities. Bless my mind, body, and soul. Amen. Keeping my chin up. Love, Nicci XOXOXOX

February 24, 2006

Dear Journal,

I had so much fun last night. Punch and I went out and had drinks all night and played pool. For everything, I only had to come out of pocket like $5. Lots of menfolk in my face. One even treated Punch and I to breakfast at Waffle House. Maybe it was because Freddy was there. He's this younger guy that lives downstairs from me. I got a little crush on him. He's cute, dark-skinned, and dresses nicely. He's a barber; he cut Dresen's hair once; that's how I met him. He wanted me to come over to his crib after the club. Guess what? I'm running for Miss X. I'm excited. I also signed up to do missionary work in India. The duration is about 3 weeks, and they'll go sometime in Oct/Nov. I forgot to tell you I got a real good internship up at xx. I started about a month ago. Now, let's talk about crazy G2. I don't feel like it, he's not worth the lead in this pencil. Anyhow, til next time, be easy. Love, Nicci

March 11, 2006

Happy Sabbath!

1 Thess 5:18, Luke 21:19, and 1 Peter 1:7. Trial of your faith. Thanks, but why, and what for? In everything, give thanks.

Dear Journal,

Made it to church this morning. God is good. I remember a couple weeks ago I prayed to God for John. (A homeless man I see quit often. If I have a few dollars to spare, I will shoot him some.) But after praying with him once, I drove off and went home. I prayed for him, I prayed for him like I've never prayed for a stranger before. John stinks. He always wears the same clothes, he's dirty and unshaven. All in all, he's a Bible scholar trapped in a cage called cocaine. I'm friendly with him because I see a trait of me in him. Anyway, when I was writing about G2 earlier, John walked in the church. He was cleaned up, shaven and with a haircut. Black, ironed pants with a white polo collared shirt. I got 2 words for you, Journal: Praise God! On this beautiful, sunny, holy, Sabbath Day! With Love, Nicci XOXOXOX

March 25th, 2006

Dear Journal,

Happy Sabbath! Well, well, well, I know I haven't been talking to you like I usually do. I've started writing my business plan. In another notebook. All in all, I'm blessed to be in church this gorgeous Sabbath afternoon. This week I found out I have a semi-large cyst on my left ovary. I've been experiencing these severe lower abdominal cramps. I had a full-scale exam last Thursday by a man! Will call him Jai. I think he fancied me. When no one is around, he calls me by my first name. When nurses, techs, or anyone else is around, he calls me Miss xx. He's a little flirtatious. He was extremely adamant about me using birth control pills and condoms. He even called me last night just to repeat the same things over again to me. Occasionally, he'd stop and there would be a brief silent pause in our conversation. He's sweet, I've never had a doctor find interest in me. It's refreshing. I am doing

119

okay; Big Dogg is my best friend. He is always there for me. To boost me up when I'm low, to encourage me when I'm discouraged, and he brings joy to a sorrowful day. Aside from Mary Jane, I must thank God for him.

March 29th, 2006

Dear Journal,

Indeed, my good, good friend. You know it's been like a while and I have plenty for your ever-so-hungry pages. Let's start with me. Big Dogg is not the joke I thought. His whole game is for real. The whole operations are real sticky. It's like a close look into the underground guys' mind. How they think. Where they come from. Why do they all think that selling weight is the only answer? Journal, it's so sad, sickening me to my stomach! A young dealer, 17 was shot in the face yesterday. I also found out that my neighbor (white, around 40) died recently in a car accident. No wonder I haven't seen her truck in a while. It's sad, Journal, sad. I don't like this feeling, not one bit. "Got this situation up in my hands, going along with some bogus plans." Lord, You know I'm a little scared; don't save me, just make me prepared. Be my armor to protect my flesh and to keep me at my best. When the fire causes the heat to rise, Lord, protect me, and keep my eyes at the skies. Shepherd me, lead me and invade my body with love. Amen. Journal, G2's rusty self! You know that peasant (forgive me, Lord!) man is a thorn in my flesh! I haven't been talking about him too much recently because You and I know its 99.9% going to be something foolish. We were doing okay for a while until something stupid happened! After that, this happened…… Ring… Ring… Ring (my phone)

Me: Hello

G2: Hey, you will not believe what happened…

Me: Oh, what?

G2: V's little brother was murdered.

Me:

G2: Hello?

Me: Sorry to hear. WHAT ARE YOU STILL DOING TALKING TO HER?!!!

G2: Her little brother just died!

Me: I SEND MY CONDOLENCES, BUT WHY IS IT THAT EVERYTIME SOMETHING HAPPENS IN V'S LIFE, SHE CALLS YOU?

G2: Where is your heart? You have a brother too!

Me: I send my condolences (G2 cuts me off)

G2: I can't talk to you right now.

I hung up on him.

Today, he calls, I answer. He started with some foolishness like, "Where is your heart? She just lost her brother. The first thing…" I cut all that shift stuff real short, "Are you going to the funeral?" I asked. He beat around the bush, I persisted, and eventually, he grew some nerve and said with a big boy front, "Of course I am!" (Click) INTERMISSION. Journal, I don't want you to think that I'm cold-hearted. There is a history between G2 and V. They were together for like 4 years and though she lives in Chicago, they still manage to sleep together. Journal, you know I have a BIG heart. But that whole thing just doesn't sound right. Someone dies every month in his circle (it used to be every 2 weeks); it doesn't sound right. Why does he have to go there? You're an ex-boyfriend that lives in xx. Don't you have someone else? Why is he always running to her aid? There's still something there, I know it is. Besides, he couldn't ask me. I THOUGHT I WAS YOUR GIRLFRIEND! DO HOW I FEEL MATTER? WHY ARE YOU GOING TO AN EX'S FAMILY FUNERAL? WHY? WHY? AM I SUPPOSED TO BE SYMPATHETIC? FEEL SORRY FOR HER? SHOULD I WANT MY BOYFRIEND COMFORTING HER!!!???? AN EX-GIRLFRIEND!! DOES THAT SOUND RIGHT? DOES IT? PLEASE SOMEBODY, ANYBODY. NO! NO, THAT DON'T SOUND RIGHT! PERIOD. Stop trying to switch it up. Hold on, I need a break to cool down because I am shaking, let us make a subject change. It hasn't even begun, Journal; I took my good friend to the death clinic (abortion station). The world is a cold, sad, lonely, hateful place of pain, heartache, and catastrophes with emotional break downs. Oh, please don't forget about the Drug Beast. He's ugly. They engulf! They engulf me, the world and my environment. My bad memories, lonely, drunk, crazy and high nights. I shouldn't be here. Those words jump around and drown them with whatever. Those dancing figurines. My daddy says don't collect them, there's no need. I should collect memories, not figurines. Lord, please forgive me of my sins. Lord, I'm only human. Love me, mold me I want to be a child, a real child of Yours. Lord, please give me one more time. Love, Nicci

April 7, 2006

Dear Journal,

I got a lot to say today. Did you read my freestyle with Big Dogg? Well, basically, I called up Y a couple nights ago. What had inspired me to call was because he told me the Wednesday before last that he was going to V's little brother's funeral. Anyway, I already discussed that so, when I called up Y, Big Dogg found out that SHE was, to her, his girlfriend. She had said that they had discussed marriage and they had been together for the past 8 to 9 years. She went on to tell me how many women he done gone through during the entire time of their "union." Her complaints sounded much like mine. Journal, I knew it was something. I just, I don't know. Oh well, things happen. I said to myself. It's been about 2 weeks now since I've seen him. Every time he calls, I'll say something rude and evil to him. But he keeps calling. I even bad mouth his momma. I figure this, him and all that he is about is a game. I like playing games, don't get me wrong, but when it's something trifling, I can't even get down like that. He can play by himself, I quit! Besides that, school is breaking my neck, and this pageant has got me all stressed out. I'm so nervous. The dance routine, my poem, and I need another gown, I think. Oh, God, be with me and S; she's going through it. Anyway, let's talk about him, what should I call him? I need a nickname. I like, "Refresh." Yes, I like that. Anyway, his name is Jai.

CHAPTER FIVE

Paradigm Shifting

God was gradually working on my mind. You know that saying of if you take one step, He will take two? That's what was happening exactly. I found that the more I made progress to change, the enemy was right behind me nipping at my heels. During this time, I would constantly have the same dream. In the dream, I was running, running for my life from this black dog with red eyes. No matter how fast I ran, he was always right behind. Hundreds of nights, the same outcome; me running full throttle. Funny thing is that he never caught me.

***** *

April 16, 2006

Dear Journal,

I feel so weird right now. I almost kissed JJ today. It wasn't like I meant to; it came from my subconscious. I know it did. It's something I've never told you before. I look at other girls. It's horrible. I catch myself checking out other girls. It's a nasty and evil monster hidden inside of an emotion or corrupt feeling that I'm going to starve to death and kill. God, take it away and give me strength to overcome it. To that list, please add: smoking, cursing, Mary Jane, lying, gossiping, and more faith in You. Subject Change. Anyway, Sabbath was beautiful, but I got some old emotions from the past. So, it was a dent in my weekend. (Having to leave xx) Today was a little better. I hadn't smoked in a whole week, but my cousin shot me some and Big Dogg brought some. I noticed a lot of foolishness today. First JJ came to town. Well, to make a real long story short, I caught vibes of jealousy, rudeness, and just hater juice–distant like, but fake too. I just wanted to hang out with anybody; she was in town, called and we chilled. I know deep down she is not my real friend. Oh, well, now let's discuss what

Big Dogg did. My so-called homeboy. He picked up me and my friends (N was there), and he started driving all crazy and reckless. When I mentioned something about it, he rudely and coldly blew me off. I was kind of hurt, he was supposed to be my good friend. Why would he, how could he bluntly disrespect and coldly talk to me. I thought about the X pill he tried. He told me it was his first time doing it, and his whole high made him feel like superman. He mentioned that he feared getting addicted to it. He added that he wasn't going to try it anymore. But tonight, he acted like he might have been high on one of those X pills. I don't care to have him in my life no more. He offended me, and I don't need any friends like that. All in all, God is plainly showing me all my so called "friends." Loneliness creeped in and out of it; I see this! Between You and me, I don't have any real friends. I see You, God! I'm going on a month now without having sex. Are You proud of me? I've decided that sex is not a necessity for me to just being with someone for only that. Plus, I need to be with someone trustworthy. You feel me? Anyway, God Bless, Good night. Love, Nicci XOXOXO

April 22, 2006

Dear Journal,

Feliz Sabbados! I'm at xx and pleased to be here. I've had a pretty good week. I've been working out all week. I must have walked at least 15 miles in the past 5 days. The weight room manager has started training Punch and me. My body is extremely sore, but it's for the best. My pageant is on Thursday. I can't wait to get this over with. I really, really, really hope Jai is going to be there. I pray that nervousness doesn't take me. I need this award money to pay for school this summer. If a woman could ask God (her heavenly Father) for a gift, please grant me this one. God Bless, Love, Nicci

Dear God,

I hear Your voice. You speak to me in my thoughts. You're so good to me. You asked me why I think I'm not worthy. I say, because to me, I'm nothing, Lord. Nothing but a smoker, curser, liar, and fornicator. You say, "Good! I can't work with anybody that is perfect!" But why me? God says, "because I love you." Lord, I'm tired of letting You down. I'm tired of having a little faith. Lord, continue to work in my life; I'm going to get right, Lord. I'm trying. Help me in this pageant. Lord, keep nervousness away and at bay. Bless me with a spiritual confidence. Lord, direct my footsteps and words. Help me not to embarrass myself. Lord, not my will, but Thy will be done. Even if I don't win, I want to at least have tried my best. Thank You for granting me this beautiful opportunity. I know You're able, Lord, and You're the real judge. Not man. If I have found favor in Your eyes, that's what matters to me. Lord, Punch wants me to go out with her tonight. I don't want to because I've moved on somewhat from those places. But anyway, put a stumbling block between it. I know I lied, but I just didn't want to go; but I told her I would. I'm tired of being a liar. IM TIRED OF BEING A LIAR! (I always do that, making false promises. Help me to overcome that, Lord.) Thank You for my life, health, strength, material possessions, and my new Razor phone. (I've wanted one for so long!) Please send a suitable person my way. God bless, Love, Nicci

April 27, 2006

Dear Journal,

Pageant Day! I'm a little uneasy, but not as bad as earlier. After I prayed, the butterflies went away. I'm only fretting over 2 things. 1-the dance routine and second, my talent. Lord, I hope and pray that I don't fall, trip, stutter, or do any type of mess up. Be with me, Father, keep my confidence and self-esteem at an all-time high. I know You're able, Lord; guide me! Lead me, Lord. Z is just for the heck. G2 can't get right, but I won't wait. Drew, I just don't know. B is a showoff and Jai, who knows. I called him last night at about 8 pm. I haven't talked to him in a minute, it's been about 2 weeks. After our little conversation, he thanked me for calling to remind him. Well, Journal, it is getting time, so pray for me! Love, Nicci

May 7, 2006

Dear Journal,

Hey, how are you? I'm not doing too well today. I done caught me another monkey on my back. I'm just trying to maintain. One word that comes to mind, Loneliness. Old memories have been haunting me since Friday. Today is Sunday. My mother and my father, sister, brothers, grandparents, friends, everybody: I don't feel like being bothered by anybody. Bad memories are like scars on your body. Every time you look at them, you think of how you got them. I love my mother; I love her dearly. Each time I investigate her face, I feel her, herself. There isn't a thing in this world I wouldn't do for her. Journal, she's hurt me. She's hurt me bad. As a teen and pre-teen, life was a struggle. I don't really know how to put it into words, but it was hard, and I'm going to try to share it with you. As a child, my life was near perfect. Both my parents had good jobs. Their annual income was close to six figures. Christmas and birthdays were always on point. I used to get lots of new school clothes when September rolled around. I can still smell breakfast in the morning. We were strict vegans. Sabbath morning: Christian music would be turned on, my mother making breakfast, my brothers fighting over something stupid, and me, I had an all-pink room. Pink walls, pink carpet, a 5-piece cherrywood bedroom set, many toys, a couple neighborhood friends, life was good. We used to camp and fish a lot. That's how it was back in the 907. I learned how to dip net, snag, bait a line, tie a line, set up a tent, build a fire, chase bears and moose away, all kinds of things like that. Sometimes we'd go with other members from our church. We'd have a ball, so much fun. We had chickens, cats, dogs, puppies, rabbits, peacocks, ducks, geese, lizards, fish, hamsters, chinchillas, turtles, everything a pet store would sell, we had it. My parents were rich. Whatever I needed, I got. Just like that. Life was perfect. At 9, I got baptized. By who, you ask? My father, he was an elder in the church. When I went down into the watery grave and came back up, I was a new 9-year-old. I felt different. Even to this day, 15 years later, I can remember that feeling. I felt perfect. Sinless, if you may. Kind of angelic. I felt so pure, and God was there. How do I know this? I felt Him. To feel God around me at the time...nothing could ever go wrong. Peace. That's it, I felt peace. My mother delighted the family with news of a baby on the way. My dad felt so good that he bought my brothers and me some brand-new bikes. I was living in a dream. My parents loved secondhand stores. On one family day, we went shopping. My brothers and I headed for the toy section (as always). Journal, that was my last day. My childhood went out the window. Peace left and confusion replaced it. Joy moved out and despair in. My mother went off, and loneliness took her place. You know, being a kid, in your own kid world, grownups have their own things going on.

They try to hide things from us but we're not completely oblivious. I know I wasn't. I peeped game real early as a child. My mother started bleeding. Dad dropped us off at Grandmas. We lived with her for a few weeks or months I guess, but it seemed like forever. They'd call, but…Dad picked us up and back to the Valley we went. I remember he told me about the baby. Mercy was his name…at 7 months gestation, he had died. I began to cry. At the time, I really didn't understand. But since mom was crying, I cried too. She quit her job for a while and just laid around. She didn't really cook no more. But dad took her place as best as he could. Some more time went by. Money started getting tight. My Christ-loving parents turned, changed. Dad turned kind of mean and Mom, aloof. It hurts, Journal. It hurts a lot. My nose is starting to tingle, and my eyes are getting heavy. What should I tell you next? It gets worse. I tell you, Journal, it hurts. Confusion, yelling, fights, food shortages, what should I say next, Journal? What do you want me to say? I can feel my emotions. Mom stopped going with us to church (something happened between her and Grandpa; she went to him for some money and he tried to take advantage of her, allegedly). Some more time passed. I was about 11. Mom was heavily dependent on prescription drugs and crack. Valium, Tylenol 4's, Mepograms, things like that. She'd sleep a lot and was always drunk acting. By now, Tia was in the picture (my baby sister). During this time, all the family's responsibility fell on Dad. He was the strong one. Mom got to him, too. He started using too sometimes, I think. Jahne went to live with Grandma and Grandpa. You see, Jahne was…. In my mother's missionary days, she went to Central America to adopt a baby. She returned with Jahne, a 6-week-old Spanish-looking baby. I loved him. One the other hand, he had extreme special needs. He was epileptic, slow, and he did crazy things. Like killing little kittens, touching girls inappropriately, lighting fires, etc. Mom and Dad were going through a lot already. They made me depressed. It was so much. I lived in my room…reading and listening to music. Oh, and school. Money was tight. Very tight. They sold stuff, pawned stuff. TVs, VCRs, my bedroom set, our animals. New school clothes became a distant memory. Mom's duties fell on me. Cooking, cleaning, diapers, washing clothes, doing Tia's hair, etc. She would sleep all the time in her room, coming out only rarely to start a dispute with my father. Dad would yell and spank us a lot. For anything.

May 14, 2006

Dear Journal,

1 Samuel 1:9-11. Today is Sunday. Yesterday I was honored to witness my parents' baptism…to see my mom and dad go down into the watery grave. Jahne and Tia followed. Oh, and by the way, I played AF out the frame. I must have gotten at least $800 from him. My justification: he was trying to play me, so I got him first. Who? What girl in her right mind would cut AF? He's weak, this isn't the first time I've done this to him. Right now, I'm at G2's church. Don't start with the questions, I already know what you're going to say, so cut it. I'm enjoying myself. The sermon? You need friends. God puts us on the earth for each other. Hannah believed in prayer. Which led to the birth of Samuel. Don't beg God, ask Him. Everything gone be alright. Hanna left Samuel with Eli in the temple. Eli got old and couldn't light the oil lamps. Samuel could! lol

May 20, 2006

Happy Sabbath!

Get Behind Me

Men use me. They don't give me money out of the simple kindness of their hearts. But they say they do. I'm a single woman. No job, no money. These men use me. Their motives are impure. After giving me a great deal, he'll ask, "want to spend the night?" I go from one man's whore to another. I'm a harlot, drinker, curser, smoker, liar. Last night, Big Dogg and I got a bottle then went to Doc's house. Got high as ever. I felt bad. AF kept blowing me up, G2 too. I just don't care anymore. These thoughts and reflections are dancing in my head. I've been in school for 6 years and haven't graduated yet. Get behind me, Satan. I'm so lonely. By myself a lot. Big Dogg is my only friend. I don't want to be here no more. Get behind me Satan.

I wanted to feel You in this place,

And with amazing grace, the warm sun touched my face.

Then, a soft hand of wind blew my hair;

Suddenly, I was without a care.

Now, I wanted to see thee.

A pair of butterflies danced before me.

The clouds sky walked slowly.

Gentle raindrops fell sporadically.

A colorful rainbow glowed magically.

Now, I wanted to hear thee,

And a chorus of birds sang a melody;

Crickets played a harmony.

June 1, 2006

Dear Journal,

Well, it has been a few days since we've last spoken. For real, I didn't have anything worthy to write about. Well, at least in my personal life. Well, well, well, where and what? So today I found out that my mom's new dr. is Jai. He asked her about me today! I feel so...no, refreshing. I'm glad I've got something new to occupy my thoughts. I don't really know what goes on in his head, but I can say that I felt vibes coming from him during the visit. He seemed a little uneasy. He would repeat questions, look at me funny, and seemed to be slightly flustered. He only called twice with a doctor tip. I figured he was kind of like, lame, but in a sweet, cute way. Since he kind of fit the profile: dark, doing something with his life, not ignorant or country acting. Honest, compassionate, and sweet. (He's not short either.). I used to call him at least once a week or every other week; just to show a little interest and shoot the breeze with him. Besides, he's a good phone conversationalist. But he would never call me. I know he had access to my number. After a couple calls, I stopped. Figured it was all in my head. Momma goes back in 3 weeks. I hope he will inquire about me.

Love, Nicci XOXOX

June 2, 2006

Today, earlier this morning, I was at my grandma's house landscaping a piece. She had asked me if I would plant some flowers for her, and she'd give me $500. WOW! I thought, enough to pay bills. Praise God! Praise God! Thank You, Jesus. I'm so sick of G2. If I couldn't pay bills, I'd have to deal with his mess. But now, thank You, Jesus, I don't have to. I'm telling you, Journal, I'm changing. I see him now, Journal. I see him. This is the second time. I'm on my way into the pearly gates. Aside from that, thank You, God, for paying my rent. He knows I'd rather be on my hands and knees in dirt planting than dealing with G2. ANY DAY. Thank You. Praise God. Lord, You're good. Thank You for letting me win 2nd runner up and Miss Talent at my pageant. I went home with flowers, a plaque, a certificate, a scholarship and a pretty trophy! Seven other girls went home with nothing. Thank You, Jesus. For even giving me the opportunity to do something like that. Keep working on, my God! Help me to stop smoking, cursing, drinking, and living a bad lifestyle. Keeping my eyes on God, Love, Nicci XOXOXO

June 9, 2006

Dear Journal,

My day has been a little stressful. I woke up at like 5:45 am and cleaned the house. Called my grandma at 7:30 am. Was at her house by 10:30 and worked like a slave on her yard in 95-degree weather for 2 long, sweaty hours. I was really looking forward to my mom seeing Jai this afternoon at 1 pm. Supposedly, he said he wanted to talk to her about a comment she had made regarding her calling him her future son-in-law. Today, she said she was having a bad day and couldn't talk to him because she was rushing to get out of his office. I strongly believe that she is lying about the whole thing. I bet he didn't ask her about the pageant, or me, or even the mannerisms he displayed. She even said that he might be gay. Then, she said something was going on between him and another staff member. Right now, I'm so irritated, I could really care less about the whole situation. I'm just going to pull out my game card and charge this whole frenzy to the game. I can't stand talking to her. She mumbles, slurs, doesn't let me talk, gets off the subject at hand numerous times, and always exaggerates the story. She has been this way for years, and that's why we don't have a relationship. She isn't consistent. And is forever negative about everything. Oh, how she irritates me so. Love, Nicci

June 10, 2006

Dear Journal,

Praise God! Glory, glory! Thank You, Jesus, Praise, praise thank You Jesus! For waking me up this morning Lord and giving me breath in my lungs. The ability to walk, talk, and my health. Thank You for giving me this beautiful Sabbath. Thank You, Jesus. He's brought me so far. Too far from where I've started from. The abundance of food in my kitchen, my bed I sleep in, bills all paid! I do not even have a job yet and yes; He is shown mercy upon me. My supporter, provider, creator. Thank You, Jesus, for everything. My family, car, apartment, and I even got my hair and nails done. Glory! Glory! Thank You, Jesus, you been too good. Mercy. My heart leaps about in my chest. My blood pressure is rising and the cells in my body cry out. Silently, they are singing, "Holy, holy, oh God, how mighty." He's coming one of these days. He is going to come back and take me unto Him. For where he is, I shall be also. Thank You! Love, Your struggling, but humble and always faithful servant, Nicci XOXOXOX

June 13, 2006

Dear Journal,

I can still feel it. I know you can. My plant business is about to pop off. God is making a way for it. Oh, and by the way, I'll start propagating and micro-propagating philodendrons along with other tropical and exotic plants. I'm hoping to get into this house off xx Rd. Guess what? The house is yellow! My favorite color. 2 stories, 3 bedrooms, 2 bathrooms, a den and a utility room and don't forget the spacious back yard. I plan on converting the downstairs into a lab/nursery. I need money though. But I feel it's going to get somewhere important. It's a ministry. God created plants for us. To teach us a lesson of Him, through them. Brainless creatures that depend solely on God. All they pretty much have is cells. Their cells respond to God. Cells, if they can listen and know, I, who have a brain, can listen too. Love, Nicci XOXOXOXO

June 18, 2006

Dear Journal,

Yesterday I went to camp meeting for Sabbath worship. That morning I had lollygagged for a little but quickly got myself together in my white, flowing, summer sundress. As soon as I pulled up on campus, my heart started to wildly beat. I felt joy and was happy to be there. I parked and headed to the tent to meet my entourage (family). Church was a blast. I had a wonderful and marvelous time. I felt God. Aside from P trying to leave her baby with me. We were all excited and P drives up "Nicci, you going to your grandma's house?" "Ya," I reply. Her, "I'll see you over there." My entourage caught it and told me to dismiss crazy on wheels before she gets to Grandma's house.

(Grandma is totally against folks inviting themselves to her house.) at grandma's house, P has her friend knock on the door and ask my grandma to warm up something in the microwave. Then a van full of people roll up in the driveway. My whole family came down on me like a flood. "Tell your friend…!" or "What is wrong with her?" A whole lot of things happened, and I asked my mom to come and my aunt volunteered. Mom didn't come for whatever reason. So outside I went to tell P and her whole posse that she was not invited to come eat. S was with her. S is normal. Something rude came out. I don't remember exactly what it was, but P and S were like, "Wow, Nicci, that was kind of harsh." I didn't really care about what P felt, but I did take S aside and quickly explain to her that my family didn't care for P too much. She said she understood, and I apologized. My aunt wasn't doing too much, but then my dad came out like Superman, took me and P aside, and tactfully told P she wasn't invited, and neither were her friends. They left. I was so frustrated and upset, I started fussing at my Dad as to why he came out instead of mom. He is always there. When will Mom? Maybe her shift is up or maybe she's on break. Anyway, we get in the house, and they all let me have it again. I felt uncomfortable. All this was not my fault in the least; it was P. As I was trying to plead my case, Nicci started shrinking. I felt bad. Bad for S, P, and the van full of my fellow brothers and sisters in Christ. *Why not?* I silently asked myself; we have plenty of food here. Aren't we supposed to be Christians? Journal, we just got out of church. Would God have turned them away? No, but my grandparents sure did. The comments, suggestions, accusations, and opinions were closed with a sideways verbal from my semi-evil Grandpa. Instantly, I wanted to leave. But my rumbling belly said no, so I gave heed. Then, T my cousin starts with her immature teasing about my hair and chest. Jahne entered the kitchen (one of my little brothers who is 18). His craziness puts P's to shame, for real. He was going through one of his mood swings again. I commented on his being rude to Dad. He ignored me, and I left it alone. Aside from all this activity, I really, desperately wanted to go home. Dad said he'd take me. Then, Satan threw another monkey wrench, Jahne. As I was talking to Dad, he busts in the conversation with, "Dad, I need to talk to you." I told him that Dad was going to give me a ride back to my car. He jumped stupid with me and like a fool, I jumped too. It all ended with a screaming match (thank God it didn't turn physical) I left, we left, he left. Everybody left. The remaining highlight of my day: I went to church, paid my tithes. Yesterday I felt joy, happy, God. I also did good on keeping the Sabbath. Anyway, looking to the skies. Love, Nicci XOXOXO

June 22, 2006

Dear Journal,

LET THEM KNOW! Let them know! Who I am, what I am and where I am going! Tell them to keep on forming their weak weapons. Keep on tearing my flesh with your cutting tongue. Keep on! Silently, humbly, I'm turning cheeks, my cheeks. But soon. SSShhhh. Soon, I'm gone come up! You hear me? No, not yet of course not. You won't ever be able to hear me. But, you'll for sure see me. I'm coming up! So, LET THEM KNOW! Love, Nicci

July 1, 2006

Dear Journal,

Hey! How are you? I'm doing good. But didn't make it to church. I don't like going by myself. I go and see girlfriends with their boyfriends, husbands with their wives. Everybody seems to be there with someone. Who am I there with? Me, myself, and I. Church is so family oriented. Anyway, let's talk about my other project. Can you guess who? Jai! I had to go up to the office because those pills were making me bleed. For like 2 weeks I had my period. When I called and told the nurse what was going on, she insisted that I come in an get checked out to make sure it wasn't anything serious. So, I'm up there in the room waiting on him and the nurse to come. Journal, I was so nervous I kept trying to leaf through a magazine, but my hands were trembling. I couldn't believe it. After 3 months, I'm about to see him again. Soon, I heard his voice and it was getting closer; these sounds sent my blood racing throughout my body. The anticipation was killing me, and a part of me was scared. I didn't want to make my crush look obvious. Now, knocking. I didn't answer, but he and his nurse came in. I tried my best to avoid eye contact but snuck a peek or two at him. To my surprise and disappointment, he was kind of fussy. He wanted to know why I wasn't dressed out, how many pads I was going through a day, and where I was this morning for my appointment. His attitude helped me forget about my crush and soon, I was snapping back at him. I kept looking at him like he was crazy because that's how he was acting. It was like he completely forgot about our past conversations regarding my medical situation. While he was showing out, I kept thinking, 3 months for this? I can't believe I liked him! He's not even that cute, and he's so not fresh. He even looked different. Instantly, I felt stupid and I wanted to leave. It got to a point to where I was a little mad. Thinking to myself, I'm a dime! A dime! And look at him. A brief exam followed, and they left to get something. Siting in the empty room, I crossed my legs and waited to get my blood drawn. Jai returned by himself. I looked up at him, and I could tell his demeanor changed and his voice was lower. While he was asking me a series of stupid questions that I know he already knew the answer to, I was searching his eyes for a window. I can't say if I saw one or not. The nurse came in and we (me and Jai) shared some words that to my own ears sounded like, I don't know. So, I continued, she took my blood, he escorted me to a chair. He sat in one (in front of the computer) and I sat in the one next to him. He was trying to log-in on something repeatedly and me, I was looking at him, but if he started looking at me, I'd look away as if I wasn't looking at him at all. I noticed everything about him. Oh no, my crush came back and soon I was feeling it again. When his nurses are around, he shows out; but when it was me and him, he was okay. He gave me a pack of pills, scheduled another appointment, and called for his nurse to check me out. He kept standing around and every now and then would ask me a question. "Are you sure my nurse didn't call and remind you of your appointment?" (They did). "You take vitamins?" He also asked. He even told the nurse how to correctly spell my name, and he remembered the exact day that I was last in the office. So, I left after she was done. Over the next 3 days, I tried to get my blood test results, but the nurse wouldn't call back, was busy, or I'd miss their call. After Thursday night, I refused to call up there anymore. Guess who called Friday morning? Jai! His voice was the first one I heard that morning. He didn't have to call but did. He apologized for waking me and asked some MD questions. But sometimes he goes blank, and there will be a long silent pause in the conversation. "Thank you, Jai," I closed the rap with saying it as sweet as Jane or Marilyn would, and that was it.

Love, Nicci

July 23, 2006

Dear Journal,

Well, I haven't talked to you in a while. That's because I've been just so busy. I moved into a new apartment. It has 3 bedrooms, 1½ baths, hardwood floors and no frig, washer, or dryer. Please pray for me, Journal; my parents live a couple of buildings away, and I've been living off them for the past 3 weeks, and to top it off, I haven't been to church in 4 weeks. You know what they say; bad news first, then the good. But on a better note, I haven't smoked in like almost 3 days. Aren't you proud of me? I know I sure am! Also, God and I are getting closer; He's allowing all this to happen so I can get closer to Him. Nowadays, I pray 3 to 4 times daily. Every time my erratic emotions start to conquer me, I call His main line and I call collect, He accepts, and I tell Him what's going on. I feel like I'm getting better. Glory! Glory! Thank You, Jesus, SUBJECT CHANGE! On last Friday, I just had to holla at my crush. So, I got up my nerve and called up to his office.

Her: Hello?

Me: Jai, please

Her: May I ask who's calling

Me: Nicci

Her: One moment, please.

Then the hold music came on. But Journal, suddenly, I went dumb and my nerve failed. I thought to myself, *what am I going to say to him? I'm going to look and sound stupid.* So, in return, I hung up while still on hold. To top it off, I turned my phone off and went to sleep for a couple hours. That was a hectic day. Anyway, it wasn't going to get any better. So, taking a nap to wake up and start over was my best bet. Six o'clock rolled around, I woke up and went to Walmart. On the way, I checked my messages, seven new ones! Guess who one belonged to? Jai! To hear his voice on my voicemail sent me stupid! I almost had a heart attack. This is what he said: "Um, Miss Nicci, this is Jai returning your call. Call me back at xxx-xxx-xxxx, thank you." You see, Journal, there are a few things to take note of: I called him at 1:57. And he called me back at 2:37. He also gave me a different number to call him back on. Next, I called the number and it rang twice, then it went to a faxing noise. I can't believe that! How is he going to play me like that? So, I called my voicemail to recheck the number again, and then guess whose incoming call came in? guess who? Jai's!!!! *What?* I thought. He called exactly three minutes after I called the fax line. I was a little bit more relaxed and told him that I just called to say what's up. Then he asked me how my summer was going, and we chatted casually for about 10-15 minutes. It was almost 9 pm, and he said he had to go and lock up, so he told me to be good and stay out of trouble. I told him to be good. He laughed, I laughed, and we hung up. So, you think he likes me? Anyway, be good and God Bless! Love, Nicci XOXOX

July 30, 2006

Dear Journal,

I got a little bit of bad news. I slept with G2! Only because I just felt plain obligated. I've been going on like 3 weeks without a frig, washer, or dryer. After he stole my keys and phone, I was finished. But he brought the appliances over and stressed it. So, like a stupid girl, I gave it up. Soon after, felt guilty as hell. I was mad at myself. I was angry. Journal, I hate him with a passion. For real for real, I just did it for some grocery money ($200). Can you believe that? I felt so bad. I felt dirty. As soon as he left, I fell on my knees and asked God for forgiveness. Not only forgiveness, I repented to never, ever, ever let it happen again. Since then, God forgave me, but it's even harder to forgive myself. He (God) loves me so much, Journal. Even after I made him my husband. I cheated! Wow, what an awful feeling. To top it off, if Jai knew, he would probably be disgusted with me. Grandma says I'm never going to find a decent man to love me because of the way I carry myself. But between you and me, Journal, I was starving. I was tired of living off my poor parents. I had been eating tuna out of a can. I know I should have stood fast, but the hunger pangs hurt. G2 makes me feel like a quarterson. If there are ever going to be readers of this book, never ever say what you won't do. My creator forgave me and later that night, after serious prayer, I forgave myself. Satan loves to whisper these past events in my ear, but I just shun him by keeping my eyes on God and the blessings He's bestowed unto me. I try not to think of my cup being ½ empty, out loud, I cry in my apartment, "Its ½ full! Thank You, Lord, for loving me!" Thank You, Lord, for loving me! And forgiving me. What keeps me strong? Praises! Every time I get depressed about life, I start praising God. For whatever comes to mind. If one of my plant seeds sprouted, I look at it as a miracle and start rejoicing. Every meal, my praise goes up! Even if it is just a can of tuna. Because there are people who don't even have that. My bed, clothes, shoes, even if they're old and worn. I praise God for them. I still haven't smoked any Mary Jane or cigars, or drunk alcohol; and I'm going strong. God is my strength. Whom shall, I fear? I look up to Job. I want to be like him. Loyal to God. I figure, even if I mess up, I'm still going to have God's praise on my lips if there is breath in my lungs! Praise God! Keeping my chin up! Love, Nicci XOXOXO

July 31, 2006

Dear Journal,

Not much to say today. I kind of stumbled last night. Let me share it with You. I've been pretty much locked up in the house for a while. I haven't gone nowhere because of my money situation. It slipped my mind how people respond to me. I'm not trying to sound conceited, but I am a beautiful girl. (Praise God!) It felt good to go out again. T and I went to see Pirates of the Caribbean, and then we went to her homegirls house and played a couple hands of spades. It was nice to get out of the house and have a girl's night out with some acquaintances. I even picked up a Sunday newspaper, so I can possibly find a job that will work with my school schedule, my Sabbaths, and that'll pay decent so I can support myself. I don't want you to think I'm anxious but....15 more days til my appointment with Jai. This is going to be my last appointment with him, and I hope something gets popped off. Wish me luck! Love, Nicci XOXOXO

August 2, 2006

Dear Journal,

Well, well, well, let's be completely honest with ourselves. Fantasy seldom becomes my reality. Jai is a fantasy. I don't know what my problem is. Yes, I do. I'm lonely. He barely flirts with me and I only talk to him like once every other blue moon. He's not seriously interested in me. Besides, he's probably got just as much baggage as G2. I believe that I blow his actions out of proportion. It is a known fact; he doesn't like me as much as I like him. I'm thinking about not even going to my appointment on the 15th. Why? What for? To find out if that cyst is still there? To pay scarce money for a mouthful of emptiness. What do you think? Any advice for your girl? I'm just plain discouraged. I'm going to be 24 next month, and who will I marry? I wonder, does God want me to marry? Has he got someone for me already picked out? I think he does because in the Word it says that He knows the desires of our hearts. I'd love to be married. I wonder what my husband is going to look like. I wonder about his hair, hands, his scent and his personality. I know God's got someone picked out for me, it's just a matter of time. I just hope it will happen before I get too old. I wonder if I'm ever going to have children. My prayer tonight: Lord, bless me with a smart, funny, dark-skinned, happy, trustworthy, faithful, patient man with a nice family too. Love, Nicci XOXOXO

August 10, 2006

Dear Journal,

Hey! How are you? I'm okay. Well, let me stop lying. A couple things are bothering me bad. First, Big Dogg done totally switched up and set me up for one extreme okie dokie. It all began Saturday. No, let's start with Thursday. Grandma knew I didn't have food at my house, and

I'm not even going to mention that she owns a food bank. She wanted me to cook macaroni and cheese for a potluck she was having at her house. So, she dropped off the ingredients for the dish. A couple hours later, I heard my mother on the phone practically begging her for a food basket. Journal, I snapped and started yelling in the background of their conversation. I said for her to come pick up the ingredients and do the dish herself. I said as many times as I've slaved for her, she could at least give my poor old mom some food. I said if she didn't come pick them up, I was going to do a drive by and throw the food on her lawn. I had just finished praying and all that happened. She was wrong, and I was wrong. God, forgive me. By Friday night, I apologized. Saturday night was better. Big Dogg had called that afternoon and asked if I'd accompany him to Atlanta. Journal, I wanted to go out of town so bad, I said yes. Plus, he offered to buy me some new clothes. To make a long story short, he propositioned me to be his girlfriend. SUBJECT CHANGE. I don't like spiders. They are gross, hairy, sneaky, and they do their work at nighttime. They plan a web and start to spin it. They plant themselves right smack in the middle and wait for a victim to accidentally run into their trap. Then, monstrously they march over, wrap them up in a blanket of death and they devour them from the inside out. They do things like this all night. By morning, the web is gone, along with the victims and the predator. And no trace of anything is found. SUBJECT CHANGE. The predator befriended me and made me think he was my friend. Asked me out of town, bought me some clothes, perfume, and food. Casually, he invited me into the jacuzzi. Not to mention, an unlimited supply of drugs. And he dropped the bomb. Journal, I know you're probably thinking that I'm just over-reacting, but I know a spider when I see one. He took me off my own turf. Bought me things in vain. Tried to get me intoxicated with alcohol and pills. Dropped the girlfriend syndrome. Hounded me for sex (but didn't get any). He's already got a girlfriend (live-in) and said he would leave her for me. Three strikes and you're out! He's got six. Big Dogg and I are just a dead friendship walking. It's amazing how men's real character comes out after a year. He's turned psycho and is supposedly in love with me. Love vs Lust. Lust not love is the culprit. If a man would leave a woman for another, he would leave me for another. That's real talk, Journal. So, put that in your pipe and smoke it. SUBJECT CHANGE. I told my sister to do dishes so Mom could cook. She ignored me. I asked her to fold the mound of clothes on her bed. She ignored me. I asked her to sweep and mop, and she blew me wolf tickets. Again, Journal, I snapped. But before the snap, she got in my face with her 14-year-old skinny behind and disrespected me, yelled at me, and belittled me. I've gone out of my way for her. Whatever I had, whether big or small, expensive or cheap, I shared with her. I grabbed her by her hair, pulled her to the ground, turned her over and put her in a serious head lock, followed a nice drag by the neck to her room and put her on top of the mound of clothes on her bed. I left while she was still running off at the mouth. I felt bad. I didn't want to lay hands on anybody in that way, but she turned the stage lights on, so I performed.

September 1, 2006

Dear Journal,

Hey. I'm doing beautifully. Plus, I have got a whole lot to talk to you about. Here's a list of things I've stopped: cigars (6 weeks), pot (6 weeks), sex (5 weeks), cursing (1 ½ weeks), clubs (1 month), Big Dogg (forever!). Almost 2 months clean off pot! I'm so proud. Life is so beautiful. I'm not sure if I told you, but I am on a road to righteousness. God is so good, Journal. He has blessed me abundantly. I feel like a new creature. School has started and I'm doing pretty good in my personal life (still single). I've even changed my wardrobe. I also married God! I wore a white dress and everything. We had a little ceremony, and now I'm happy. I've been doing daily devotions and I pray at least 2 times a day. If anyone ever reads this, remember one thing: prayer and God can change anyone, anything, anybody. That's just as real as the air we breathe.

September 11, 2006

Dear God,

Forgive me, Father, of my sins and trespasses. Separate me far from inequity. Thank You, Lord, for rescuing me again. I also thank You for forgiving me. For not giving up on me. Thank You for my food, shelter, clothing, and my books. But Lord, I have one more habit. Father, I beseech thee, help me to stop smoking cigarettes. I know I'll stop. For You have delivered me from so many other things, make haste. Enhance my beauty with Yours. Enable me with the fruits of the

Spirit: joy, longsuffering, goodness, humbleness, faithfulness, gentleness, self-control, kindness, patience, and peace. Thank You for loving me and for dying on the cross for me. My debt was paid through Your righteous blood, pure from all transgression. All in all, praise God. For His mercy endures forever! Love, Nicci

October 16, 2006

Dear Journal,

How are you? I'm still doing beautifully. 3 months of abstinence, no pot or cigars and about 4 weeks with no cigarettes, and cursing is still out. Journal, I feel so good. Things are crystal clear now but occasionally they get a little cloudy. But all in all, I'm blessed. G2 is wrapped around my finger. He's after me like white on rice. But he ain't got nothing coming. It's so funny how things turned out. He is desperately trying to get back with me. But little does he realize that the boat left the dock like last year. Ha Ha. Thank You, Lord. I give You all the credit. I'm done with school in December and I graduate on May 9, 2007. So, I'm trying to finish my RN starting in January. Give it to me, Lord. I beseech thee. Everything is going well. I've been going to church every week (sorry I left You). Blessed is he that pursues after righteousness. Now, I'm not perfect, I still stumble every now and then, but praise God I'm not where I once was. I'm in love! I'm in love! I'm so in love with Jesus. lol ha-ha. SUBJECT CHANGE. Journal, I still think about Jai, my beloved crush. I have not talked to him in like 2 months, but I am going to wait til April (my recheck). I'm patient. But I must admit, I can't wait to see him again. I hope something pops off then. I've been taking vitamins, and I've been slowly gaining my weight back. So, when I see him again, I'll be on point. I'm also trying to change my attitude. I need to stop gossiping and bashing folks. I wonder if he still remembers me. If he thinks about me. I wonder what he's like. His personality. The last time I called him I was so nervous that I was extremely professional with him and in return, he was that way with me. On the other hand, I hope he is still single. I haven't had a crush like this in a long, long time. Please, God, do something. You know I've been crushing on him. Help Your daughter out, Lord. Anyway, I had a dream about him a couple nights ago. Thank You, Lord. Hey, You know what they say about all good things come from God? Well, I thank God for the dream. Thank You, Lord, Love, Nicci

October 27, 2006

Dear Journal,

Hey! I just got off the phone with Chrissy, my best friend since like 6th or 7th grade. She is doing okay. Journal, I have a dilemma. I need to desperately get rid of G2 and AF. I'm not in love with either of them; I'm only tagging them along for my own financial gain. It's wrong. I've been praying that if God could bless me so that I could be financially independent, I sure would appreciate it. On a good note, I've managed to have $650 saved up. God answers prayers. He's blessing my finances, helping me to save, and He's good. He said if I was faithful to Him, He would be faithful to me and He has. I got $9200 in financial aid towards paying for school. Praise God. I hope it all goes through because if it does, I can put some of the money aside and pay my own bills for a while, so I don't have to be bothered with G2 and AF. I got 2 baby Quaker parrots a couple days ago. Their names are Debo and Juicy. I enjoy their company. I'm currently in the process of training them. SUBJECT CHANGE. You already know what my favorite topic is, right? Don't act, I know it's yours too. Guess who? Jai (giggling). April is my appointment. I have 6 more months. I always wonder what God thinks about my crush. Is He for it or against it? Is it all a figment of my imagination? I hope not. Could we possibly be something? If I could have a one-on-one conversation with God, I'd ask Hm this: does Jai like me? What is he like? Do you think he is a good pick for me? Is he already in love with someone else? I know, Journal, you're probably thinking, out of all the things I could talk to God about, I'd pick Jai? My answer is that I think of him a lot. I don't really have anyone else in my life that I feel romantic about as him so, yes. God knows my feelings for him because He made me, and He put the feelings there. I think about it as being beautiful. All beautiful things come from God. You know what my new name would be if we get married? Mrs. Jai! Lol hahaha. These thoughts tickle me pink and spark my fancy. I have a crush. It feels good. Even if he forgot about my very existence. My crushes die hard. As You can tell it's been going on for like 7 months now and still going strong. Maybe this Journal will turn into a love story. Like the

Song of Solomon. I hope so. I want it to be, and I want to fall in love. I feel like a cornball. I want to have flowers, secrets, whispers of sweet nothings. I want it all. I just hope he's a man of God. These days, those men of men can bounce for real. I hope he likes me. Love Nicci XOXOXOX

November 17, 2006

Dear Journal,

I love the Lord, because He hath heard my cry. I remember being on welfare. I remember standing in food bank lines. I remember selling my blood plasma to make ends meet. I remember the times I cried out to my creator. When I had nothing, a King remembered me. When a smoker, curser, a thief, He thought of me. I remembered months ago, I cried to Him for to change me and to make me into the Christian woman that He created me to be. I cried for Him to take my bad habits and throw them into the depths of hell. Oh, mercy. My little itty-bitty voice, a King heard me. Journal, I stopped smoking pot. You don't understand. I've been smoking it for almost 4 years, and cigars as well. I stopped. Journal, I had the mouth of a sailor, and I stopped. Oh,

Journal, I didn't do anything, it was the power in me through a King, a phenomenal King. Lord, thank You. I'm graduating from college in December. Lord, I got into xx school of nursing. Thank You, Jesus. You have delivered me from the bondage that is within myself. Thank You, Lord. Even so, Lord, I'm not right. And You know this. Journal, you know I wouldn't lie to you, so I'm going to give you the naked truth. I've slept with G2. At least twice since the last time we spoke. And I feel bad. After I had a vow with the Almighty. Deep down, it hurts me that I could hurt my creator. It separates me from God. I feel so distant from Him afterwards. Journal, I don't even love G2. It's my wretched flesh. Desire causes me to ignore and continue my sin against God. I hate my flesh. Like an open sore it cried out and screams for iniquity. Once I've fed the demon, I'm hurt. Not physically, but spiritually and emotionally hurt. Oh, I was doing so well. And I fell. I was so strong, and I lost the battle against the enemy. But you know what is crazy. God still loves me. He forgives me as soon as I ask for it. He loves me and is quick to forgive. That's amazing. But you know what's horrible? I find it SOOO difficult to forgive myself. I feel like God has been too good to me. How can I continue to sin and hurt Him? I hurt myself too. God, a King, is my best friend. My healer, redeemer, deliverer, etc. He's everything to me. Journal, why can't I do right by Him? Lord, for the record, I'm sorry for my lawlessness, my adultery, and fornications. My lying lips and my evil thoughts. Please, Savior, help me to die to the flesh. Please, Lord, take away my sexual desires until I am married. I don't want to hurt You any more ever again. You have given me strength to cut out other bad habits, Lord, please give me strength to cut this one. Love, Your struggling servant, Nicci XOXOXOX

November 23, 2006

Oh, Lord,

Comfort me, Father, for Your child is discouraged Oh, Lord, I long to be in Your presence for attention. I beseech You, oh, Lord. Harken unto my voice and my supplication, oh, Lord. The enemy put a monkey on my back, Father; help me, oh, Lord. My heart is silently screaming out to You, Father; bless me. Oh, Lord, I live in the end times and life gets so chaotic. Bless me with strength, enhance my wisdom and slowly grant me knowledge. Oh, Lord, come by here and encompass angels around my household, oh, Lord. Shape and mold me strategically into the woman You want me to be, oh, Lord. Change me. Give me a new look; wash me, Lord, and cleanse me from mine iniquities, oh, Lord. I must be with You. You're my all and everything. Don't forget about me. Love, Nicci

January 23, 2007

Dear Journal,

I know I haven't talked to you in a while. However, I've been super busy. School is competitive and challenging. I'm constantly reading and doing homework. I'm really aiming for straight A's so I can get in the upper division of the nursing program. Also, over the Christmas break, I got a job as a preschool teacher. I've also officially dedicated my life to God. On December 16th, (I believe) I got baptized at the xx by Pastor xx. I know you're probably very joyous over the good news, but my blessings haven't stopped there. G2 has been kicked to the curb as well. I haven't seen him, or gotten any type of financial assistance from him, in I guess about a month and a half, which is for me a serious record. So many times, I prayed for deliverance from him, and the Lord blessed. Also, my savings is at $3,000 and AF is stupid too. Journal, I feel so good. But I'm not done yet. This morning at about 6 am, my alarm went off. I got up to press the snooze button and when I laid back down, I glanced in the hallway. Journal, I kid you not, and you'll probably think that I'm going crazy and seeing things, but…Journal, I saw brown sugar-colored feet in the hallway. I also saw the hem part of a robe or gown. I was still halfway sleep and I figured that I was seeing things, so I closed my eyes for a second, just to re-open them and once again seen those same pair of feet. They were still there, but they turned and slowly proceeded down the hall. Then the feet were pointed towards me. You see, Journal, at first, I thought my mind was playing a trick on me. But my mind has not played any tricks on me since I was little. Therefore, I know it must have been real. I was a little scared at first, but I got a cool notion: it was my guardian angel. God just permitted me to see his/her feet this morning. Also, I have a new crush. I'm not going into much detail this time, but if things pop off between us, I'll tell you everything; I promise. But I will tell you our name for him is Icey. Love, Nicci XOXOX

March 19, 2007

Dear Journal,

Well, I haven't talked to you in a long time. Aside from the usual stuff, I'm blessed. This week is spring break, and I've been taking it easy. I'm still rolling clean if you're wondering. I'm proud to write it too. 8 or 9 months without smoking about almost 5 months without sex and I'm chilling. G2 still pops up every now and then to try to get back together. I just think, "ya, right." It feels good to have enough power to say no and feel good about it. He tries to make it sound like I'm crazy and always says that I need to seek professional help. But you know, the Bible says that we would be looked at as radicals and man would think we're crazy. But to break it down, I just listen to God and follow His commandments (or at least I'm trying to). School is stressful. I'm not sure if I'm going to get in the program; it still doesn't look too promising. But you know what they say: "Through God all things are possible." We'll see. In the meantime, I think I'll take a CNA class this summer through the American Red Cross. I also have been praying for a house. One that is paid in full. I'd love to live in a house. I'm thinking about quitting my job at the daycare because I'm always sick. Those kids keep me under the weather. I'm still single. It's not necessarily a bad thing, but it sure feels like I'm a lame. Just a few more weeks until I get to see Jai again. I've heard through unreliable sources that he's gay. It makes me SOOO sad. Even though he doesn't dig me like that, I still get the biggest kick out of seeing him and being able to interact with him. I'm going to get new braids, my nails done, my face clear, new garb, and I'm working on toning up my body. The little girl inside me just squeals with giggles when I think about him. I hope he's going to be in a good mood when I see him. Love, Nicci XOXOXOX

March 25, 2007

Dear Journal,

Yesterday was so chaotic. I had woken up late and was late to church. I stayed for about an hour and a half then I went home because I was having potluck at my house. It went great. Except one thing kept bothering me. P helped me out a lot, she had K. Mom and Dad had each other. H had xx and I began to feel so lonely. The only person I had some sort of feeling about and had access to was G2. I called him and invited him to my potluck. He said he would come in about 30 minutes. Well, you already know how he operates, and he didn't show. But to make a story short, when dark fell, he showed up. To be frankly honest with you, I love G2. And I missed him dearly. We hugged and kissed for a second. But I had to take S to work, so I left him at my house and shortly returned. I saw him sleeping on the couch in the dark. Quickly, I said a prayer; "Lord, rebuke this desire from me and help me not to stumble; put a stumbling block between him and me so I don't sin. My phone rang. I got up to see who it was, and I noticed his phone. I picked it up and started to go through it. I saw Y, J, S, the numbers went on. Journal, I flipped out and basically kicked him out. I was mad, hurt from the past, jealous, just everything. I felt bad too. Then, Icey called. He is the new guy. A xx pastor. We briefly chatted for a little, then he asked if he could come over. I agreed, so he did. Nothing really happened, we just talked and watched TV. After about a half hour, he left. Journal, I get so weird sometimes. God is all I need, but I get lonely. Lord, help me to be patient, wise, and at peace with myself. Help me not to put myself in awkward situations. Help me to not be lonely and give me victory over my own flesh. Lord bless me and please, make me to know wisdom, knowledge and understanding, Lord. I need You. Thank You for answering my prayer so I didn't sin. Keep me strong. Love, Nicci XOXOX

March 28th, 2007

A confession and prayer for forgiveness. Psalms 51.

> *[1]Have mercy upon me, O God, according to thy lovingkindness: according unto the multitude of thy tender mercies blot out my transgressions. [2]Wash me throughly from mine iniquity, and cleanse me from my sin. [3]For I acknowledge my transgressions: and my sin is ever before me. [4]Against thee, thee only, have I sinned, and done this evil in thy sight: that thou mightest be justified when thou speakest, and be clear when thou judgest. [5]Behold, I was shapen in iniquity; and in sin did my mother conceive me. [6]Behold, thou desirest truth in the inward parts: and in the hidden part thou shalt make me to know wisdom. [7]Purge me*

with hyssop, and I shall be clean: wash me, and I shall be whiter than snow. ⁸Make me to hear joy and gladness; that the bones which thou hast broken may rejoice. ⁹Hide thy face from my sins and blot out all mine iniquities. ¹⁰Create in me a clean heart, O God; and renew a right spirit within me. ¹¹Cast me not away from thy presence; and take not thy holy spirit from me. ¹²Restore unto me the joy of thy salvation; and uphold me with thy free spirit. ¹³Then will I teach transgressors thy ways; and sinners shall be converted unto thee. ¹⁴Deliver me from blood guiltiness, O God, thou God of my salvation: and my tongue shall sing aloud of thy righteousness. ¹⁵O Lord, open thou my lips; and my mouth shall shew forth thy praise. ¹⁶For thou desirest not sacrifice; else would I give it: thou delightest not in burnt offering. ¹⁷The sacrifices of God are a broken spirit: a broken and a contrite heart, O God, thou wilt not despise. ¹⁸Do good in thy good pleasure unto Zion: build thou the walls of Jerusalem. ¹⁹Then shalt thou be pleased with the sacrifices of righteousness, with burnt

offering and whole burnt offering: then shall they offer

bullocks upon thine altar.

Forgive me, Lord. Nicci

***

During this break, I had moved and was slowly removing people and temptations from my life. At the time, I couldn't really articulate what was happening on the inside, but I had what I felt was a creature living in my chest. It would tell me things, give me warnings, and guidance. The more I listened to its voice, the better I did. In no way was I perfect, but the key players that fed me negative influences were leaving and/or the unhealthy connections I had were being severed.

***

August 1, 2007

Dear Journal,

It always is a pleasure talking with you again. I know it's been like 5 months since the last time, but I didn't have anything worthwhile to talk about. This time I do. I must confess; I have messed up a couple times, but not recently. I've been so busy. I've been taking CNA classes along with summer school. (I hope I pass because I'm a super lame in that department.) Plus, I've been working at the daycare again. My appointment with Jai wasn't too much to write home about either. I mean, he was cool and nice, but that was about it. Anyway, my sister had an appointment Monday, so I took her. But first, let's backtrack about 2 months. I wanted to know if he wanted to kick it, but unfortunately, I wasn't brave enough to ask yet, so I had my best friend Crissy call him. According to the convo, this is what was said (she doesn't lie):

Her: Is Jai there?

Secretary: One moment, please. Hold on

Him: Hello?

Her: Hi, Jai, this is Crissy, you do not know me, but I am a friend of Nicci's.

Him: Okay.

Her: She was wondering if you would consider the 2 of you going out for coffee or something.

Him: Why couldn't she call and ask me this herself?

Her: Because she felt a little nervous about it.

Him: Ooh, well, I can't because she's my patient; its unethical, and I could lose my license.

Her: Okay, I understand, and thank you for your time. (click)

Journal, I must admit I felt bad and good at the same time. In the end, I left it at that. Now, back to Monday. You know I wanted to just see him even if he wasn't stunting me. So here goes the story of what went down: in the waiting room I was so nervous that my gums began to ache and throb. The nurse calls us back. While in the vital signs room, I caught a glimpse of him in my peripheral vision. I didn't want to turn and look at him, so I acted like I didn't even notice. But he saw me, turned and faced my direction with a chart in his hand, acting like he was writing in it. I still didn't turn to look. Meanwhile the nurse wanted us to change rooms, so when I turned to enter the hallway, he positioned himself in my path so I would have to speak. However, he piped up and said, "Hi, how are you?" His expression told me that he remembered the friend that called him and??? Waiting in the room, he entered and began a conversation with my sister. Even though I wanted to stare at him, I didn't; but Tia and DJ said that they noticed his glances at me. He said he was waiting on a fax and would return in a little bit. As he exited, he looked at me and asked, "How are you?" I gave him the same answer. Anyway, I couldn't wait for him to return because I had to go back to work. But Tia and DJ said that when he came back to the room he asked where I was. Journal, do you think he likes me? Still praising God in the meantime. Love, Nicci

September 28, 2007

Dear God,

Thank You for deliverance. My soul rejoices in You. My inner thoughts were read and I, a sinner, was brought back from the dead. I've changed drastically and been saved miraculously. Thank You, Lord, from the bottom of my heart, and from You I will never part. Bless me, Lord, for I ask humbly for deliverance financially. Thank You for allowing me to see another birthday. For this, I praise thee. I was a caterpillar. Crawling upon my belly. I wrapped myself in a cocoon of sin, and lingered. Too weak to break loose, I cried unto the Lord. Under confusion, heartache, and shame. I cried unto the Lord. A cage of drugs encompassed around me. Out of frustration, I cried aloud unto the Lord. Halleluiah! The mercy of God harkened unto my voice. He heard me. He heard me. Saints! He heard me! Heavenly strength broke my cocoon. Unrighteousness, abominations and sin shed from me! I am blessed. Where are thine cage and ties? Blessed be the holy hand of God. For He answered me, a sinner. Glory! Glory! I have hope! Strength. Glory. Amen

April 8, 2008

Dear Journal,

Wow, it has been a long time since our last conversation; if you don't mind, I would like to take a few moments to inform you of what's been going on. Firstly, in late October, I finished the CNA training through the American Red Cross. Shortly after, I got a job at a local nursing home. Journal, I truly enjoy that job. I find it so fulfilling. To care for people who cannot care for themselves makes me feel good. It is a very humbling job, but it kind of reminds me of Christ. He was humble and he helped the sick. I have worked double time since Christmas break. SUBJECT CHANGE. I went to a prayer summit a couple weeks ago. My grandma invited me on her expense. I was surprised she asked, but I went. Oh, Journal, the Spirit touched down. In me! Remember G2? I prayed to the good Lord, for me to rid myself of him for the last time. He did it. I have no feelings or emotions attached to him. I am no longer his call girl. I'm free, free, free. I don't need his money either because God allowed me to get an educational loan for a good grip of change. I was so blessed by the experience that it changed my whole way of thinking. I'm in tears, Journal, I'm a new creature. Jesus knows me by name, I am His and He is mine. Hallelujah! God is worthy to be praised. SUBJECT CHANGE. I was fired from my job in early January. I got sick, and she said if I didn't bring in a doctor's excuse by 5 pm, she was going to fire me. I tried to reason with her because I don't have health insurance. But she didn't care. She fired me. I believe she did it because I saw another CNA abuse a resident, and I told on her; and I would do it again too because it's wrong. You see, Journal, it doesn't get any better after that. Early

January, I met up with my nursing advisor. God is good. Blessed be the holy one of Israel. My King of kings and Lord of lords has a plan for me already in sync. Thank You, Jesus. My advisor said my GPA was still not high enough and because of a couple past grades, I can't ever be in the upper division of the nursing program. My feelings were hurt, and I cried out to my God. That man's words hurt me. And, I told my master what he said. Again, today I'm sad. All my friends around me are getting their acceptance letters. In my own solitude, I tell my God, my master knows of my hurt and inner pain. But, Journal, I will yet remain steadfast and unmovable because God has promised me a plan for my life. And whatever it is, it's alright with me. Thank You, Jesus, Praise You, God! Thou art worthy to be praised. Love, Nicci XOXOXO

April 10, 2008

Yesterday I got the "sorry to tell you but you didn't make the cut" letter from the nursing program. I'm not sure if I told you, but the night before, I wrote (the Holy Spirit told me to, I think) a letter to the director of the program. Before I handed the letter in, I already had my letter. Ironically, I turned my letter into her. This was yesterday. God forgive me, but I been worrying about it ever since. Lord, help my unbelief. SUBJECT CHANGE. You know, I have been attending xx for a couple years. And for maybe a couple months now I have been interested in a certain gentleman. Lol. His name is Chum. He is dark complexioned, my height, and he's single too. I got his number from my Pop's about a month ago and I called him up. He was nice to me and encouraged me to save his number. After a few minutes, he kept clicking over to the other line, so I let him go so he could finish his business. A week and a half later, he called. I was so excited. He asked if I would help him that weekend with some church concert. I eagerly agreed. I indeed helped him and had a ball. He called later that night to personally thank me. He then invited me to a prayer breakfast the next morning. Of course, I went. That's when I met Keisha, my newest friend. Anyway, I really, really like Chum. He is a man of God, smart, intelligent, busy for the Lord and he has no kids, nor has he ever been married. The only downside is that he hasn't called me since. I called him, and he said he was going to call me back, but he didn't. So, I didn't call him after that. But he always goes out of his way to come over and speak to me. Then again, he does that with everyone based on my observations. So now, I always look forward to seeing him. I like being in the same room with him, even if it's a church sanctuary. I always wonder if he likes me. SUBJECT CHANGE. I've been fasting every Friday for spiritual renewal. Here are some of the things I pray for: my family, friends, career, relationship with God, church, behavior, and ministering to others. Love, Nicci XOXOX

April 24, 2008

Dear Journal,

Hey, it's always nice to holla at you! I've been doing okay. I want to tell you first about Chum. I had a potluck at my house last Saturday for my god sister and S's birthday. I really wanted him to come but didn't know how to go about inviting him. I intended to talk to him after church but couldn't find him. So, I had my Pops do it. Lol My Pops called and said that he was going to come. I couldn't believe it when I heard his voice in the living room. You know how you like someone a lot and when you hear their voice, it puts butterflies in your stomach? Well, that's how I felt. Being around him with everybody else gave me an opportunity to observe the way he interacts with others. He is a down-to-earth person, socializes well with my family and friends, is polite, and directed friendly conversation with me. He thanked me for inviting him, and I thanked him for coming. Afterwards, he said he'd come along with us to the nursing home to visit and minister to the residents. He ended up staying the whole time and helping my Pop and Elder xx with the program. Hahaha, how sweet. He didn't have to, but he did. While walking out to the parking lot I thanked him again for coming. (He held the door open for me.) Then he said, "Oh, I'm coming back over for cake and ice cream!" lol I was thrilled and told him I would see him at the house. Back at the house, he ate with us and cracked on my Pops for butchering one of the hymns! "Oh, How I Love Jesus." I was so happy; it was nice having him over. NEW STORY. After prayer meeting last night, he came over to the car and began to strike up a conversation with me and K. We stood around and talked for I guess 30-45 minutes. I can tell I'm getting more comfortable with being around him. He is a free spirit with positive energy. I like his dark complexion and outlook on life. He asked K and me how we met. I told him how I had prayed for some new friends and while at a prayer breakfast, she turned around and said, "Hi, my name is K and I moved down here not too long ago, and I was looking to make some friends, So I am extending my hand to you in friendship." He chuckled and said, "Well, I'm extending my hand to you two in friendship." He then shook K's hand, then mine. Lol, anyway, I thought that was kind of funny. Well, Journal, I got to go and start my day of studying for my nursing final. Wish me luck. God bless. Love, Nicci XOXOXOX

April 25, 2008

Dear Journal,

Tutu

Ducky

(My new foster kids were writing their names in you)

April 26, 2008

Dear Journal,

Yesterday was a blessing. I'm not sure if I told You, but for the past 1½ years, I've been pushing paperwork to become a therapeutic foster parent. Finally, yesterday I got 2 beautiful black girls. Their names are Tutu (3) and Ducky (7). I must admit, Journal, they are the best things who have happened to me in a while. They didn't want to sleep in their room last night, so they slept with me. It was nice to have 2 little warm bodies on both sides of me. Except for the occasional knee in my side or elbow in my neck. Lol I bathed them both before putting them down and while bathing them, the older one said, "Our mommy called us angels." I asked, "Your mommy called you angels?" Ducky also added, "Well, you are our mommy for now, and you just called us angels." It was beautiful. I had previously answered their question about why they had to take baths and I told them, "So you can smell like angels." They are great company, and they fill a void in me that I didn't realize was there. Their social worker said I would only have them for the weekend. But I'll leave it in the hands of my God. He is the great author and finisher. Lord, thank You so much for giving me of all people this blessing. It brings tears to my heart. God loves me so much, and You have truly been changing me from the inside out. I would have never imagined doing what I am now and living how I'm living now compared to how things were going down 3 or 4 years ago.

Thank You, Jesus. God bless always, and He's in control. Love, Nicci XOXOXO

April 30, 2008

Dear Journal,

I'm in love. It's a feeling that has started on the inside and burns deeply down to my soul. It's not just my heart. It's my loins and every cell in my being that just dances in jubilee when my lover whispers to me. I, in return, am beloved. I, Journal, am beloved. I, a sinner—and you and I both know my waywardness—am beloved. To my dearly beloved, as a woman of whoredoms and enslaved to fleshly desires, You saw me. Looking past my drug and alcohol habits and filthy mouth, You saw me. A peaceful voice called my name deep from within my soul. I was in a dirty strip club. You saw me. I tried to ignore Your voice, but You wouldn't let me. "Go home," You said, "you don't belong here." You saw me. A small seed was planted and in time I fought and didn't want to turn from my scum. You saw me. Eventually, my iniquities caught up with me and life began to move too fast. Face down and at my wits end, I looked up. You saw me.

Still, in my transgressions I called Your name, for no one else was there. You heard me. As I began to complain, You listened. You reminded me with past days of memory verses from my childhood. They came to my mind and a process generated. I said, "Lord, please, I beg of You, I know I'm far, far, far from You and I let the world ruin what You made. Father create in me to be the woman You created me to be. You heard me. Something strange happened, I felt shame. A feeling I haven't felt in a while. My thinking changed. I had a bizarre feeling of wanting to be in my home of old, my church. He was working on me. Barely sober, I would catch benediction. But it didn't quench my new hunger. He began talking to me and step by step, showed me the way. He's working on me. My prayers developed into pleas of deliverance from drugs, alcohol, sex, clubbing and wicked people. One by one, He gave me victory. He is working on me. I began to slowly change. My mind started to clear, my self-esteem began to rise, dreams were being created and a new outlook on life formed. He is changing me. To be continued. Love, Nicci XOXOXO

***

After some of my friends had gotten into the nursing program, I failed to get an acceptance letter. As usual, they moved on without me. One late afternoon, the burden of rejection was so heavy upon me that I cried a prayer to the Lord that I will never forget. I told Him that in my heart, I wanted to be a nurse. I shared with Him how I felt to know other people got accepted into the program. I then told Him that I see being a nurse is not what He has planned for me. I asked Him if He would take the desire from my heart to be a nurse and replace the desire with what He has for me. I told Him that I want Him to use me. Even if it was herding earth worms. I just wanted to be in alignment with Him. I ended the prayer with thanking Him in advance for hearing my pleas and I thanked Him for giving me a new trust in Him that He has something else for me. Exactly two weeks after that prayer, I got a phone call from the secretary of the nursing department at one of the other colleges. She said they have a couple of openings to start and asked if I would be interested. Even though school had started two weeks prior. She added that the professors would allow me to catch up and extend deadlines for me. I gave her an absolute yes and hung up.

You know that dance Kind David did up and down the streets of Israel when he was able to bring the ark back to its rightful people? I don't know exactly what that looked like, but the dance I did in my living room after the conversation with the secretary probably was something similar. I learned that if we die to ourselves and accept God's will in our lives instead of our own, we will win. He did not open the door to nursing school for me until I completely let go of that dream and opened my heart to receive the dream, He had for me. Almost a year had passed since I wrote in my journal and, on a good note, I was accepted into a nursing program. All my extra energy went into studying and working full time at one of the local nursing homes. I worked nights and did school with clinicals during the day. I had little time to sleep and study, but God carried me through.

***

May 4, 2009

Dear Journal,

Hey, it has been quite a long time since the last time I chatted with you. So much has gone down. Well, first, I got into a nursing program!

Praise God! I even passed the first semester of school. (The program is 3 semesters, LPN.) God is so good. Journal, I promise you, God passed me! Now, I got into the second semester. I have been praying so hard because I must take a final on Thursday and one on Monday. It's all in God's hands. I'm just going to do my best and let God do the rest. I just hope I pass. SUBJECT CHANGE! By the way, Chum and I didn't work out. I guess he lost interest in me. Oh, well. However, I did start dating a guy named Smiley. Our relationship started by me calling him. Things between us popped off right away. He gave me plenty of attention, he'd text and call me a lot. He'd also take me out too. He was so sweet. Sad to say, I began a sex life with him (God forgave me). He didn't want to commit to me. He is a pastor! Lol He wanted to keep me a secret. I guess I was blind by all of it at first. Anyway, God is beautiful. When things began to go south between us, he was talking to another girl while I was over there. I was so upset that I left. When I got home, I left again and bought a pack of cigarettes and smoked some. I cried out to God in anguish and said to Him that I knew I had backslid. But I asked Him that if he could look past my sins, read my heart and have mercy upon my afflictions and save me from my own feelings, I would really appreciate it. Well, Journal, God heard me. Not only did He hear me, but He made things happen. He lifted my spirits, freed me from my emotions and delivered me from depression. Wow, it's so amazing. Journal, even though I can't physically see God or even place a hand on Him, He's there. My best friend. All I do is go to my knees and talk to Him like I'd talk to anybody. When I mention my hardships to Him, things happen. Bills get paid, patience is given, peace comes, and fear disappears. If anybody ever reads this, I want to strongly advise You that if EVERYTHING fails and NOBODY is around and nothing is going right, try God. I promise You. My God is a God that makes things happen. By the way, I threw those cigarettes away and took myself to church to testify. God is good. Thanks again. Praise God. Love, Nicci XOXOXOX

***

I had finished nursing school and began working as a nurse in February 2010. It was a huge adjustment for me, and I was so excited to have accomplished this. I was still in disbelief that God could carry a small time, dyslexic girl into the whole realm of being a full-blown professional. I worked overtime, double-time and worked holidays. I was finally making some good money, and my lifestyle was more comfortable.

***

June 27, 2010

Dear Journal,

Wow! It has been forever since I've talked to you. I've been busy pushing. I have lots to tell you. First, I would proudly like to tell you that I am now a nurse! It feels weird saying and even thinking it. Lol on January 27th, I got the news from the Alabama Board of Nursing that I can now practice nursing as an LPN. It's not the big time RN that I'm aiming for, but it sure is close! My first two jobs, I was fired over some bogus stuff; but now I have a job as a float nurse at another nursing home. I love my job. Being a nurse is right up my alley. It's crazy how God operates. I was a CNA through nursing school, and it was a very humbling experience for me; but I would rather wipe old people's butt's and clean up puke than be a hoe any day. And that is real life truth for you right there. Aside from the good news, I have some bad news for you too. I started smoking again. I've been praying to stop, but I'm going to keep praying for deliverance. SUBJECT CHANGE. Ya, I'm still dealing with Smiley. He is still the same. I stopped the whole physical things months ago, and now we're just friends. Even as friends, he still manages to act like a moody female. I guess I just keep him around for the company. But I know that he would never take me as a wife. I take it that I'm not good enough, but whatever. I'm still praying for a hubby. One of these days, God will send me one. Well, until next time. God Bless. Love always, Nicci

May 15, 2011

Dear Journal,

Man, oh, man! It has been ages! Indeed, it has been forever since I've chatted with you. Of course, I probably won't be able to catch you up on everything, but I will try. Remember last time we chatted, and I told you that I was now an LPN and landed a third job? Well, I'm still at the same place. God has been so good to me. I recently got a promotion too. I am now a data entry/restorative nurse. So, I do not work a cart anymore. Now I have an office that I share with medical records. So, basically, I put in doctor's orders, new admissions, ICD-9 codes, and I'm supposed to head the restorative department. (I'm praying I succeed in the restorative program.) By the way, since I have two associate degrees, I really want a four-year degree. So, I applied for the xx program. I am also slowly trying to repair my credit so I can get into my own home. So, you ask about Smiley? Well, I officially kicked him to the curb late last summer. That no good, down and dirty pastor was cheating on me. My sister caught him at the movies with another girl and not only that, he lost his job, house, and life because some girls from his congregation told on him. He begged and pleaded with me, but You know how the saying goes, "Once a cheater, always a cheater." He just broke trust with me. What is a relationship if you don't have trust? But I know what you're thinking. You probably think I'm so tough. I guess in a way God has given me a lot of strength, but I did love him, Journal. To be frankly honest with you, I thought I knew he was the one. But you live, learn, and move on. He still texts me every now and again, but that's super dead. Two months ago, I started talking to Dumpy again. He's this guy I had put down for Smiley. I decided to get back in touch with him. So, we began talking and he sounded ever so happy and glad to have me back in his life. I also apologized to him for the past. He would minister to me and pray with me all the time. I wanted someone to have daily devotions with. So, I prayed to God that Dumpy would ask me to be his prayer partner. And to my surprise, he did. Then he said, "We'll pray about it." So, I prayed to God that He would show me Dumpy. Journal, God heard and answered my prayer. Strike out, you lose again. Another dud. Another Smiley; are all Christian men like this? I read between the lines of a conversation we had today, and I found out that he is addicted to pornography and women. He even confessed to it. I told him that I didn't mind remaining his friend. After a couple of hours of thought and discussing it with my grandma, I decided it wasn't a good idea. So, I did the unthinkable, Journal. I sent him a breakup text. Lol. I know, right? Anyway, I'm not too bummed out about it because thy Maker is thy husband. Love, Nicci XOXOXO

March 19, 2012

Dear Journal,

While I'm writing this to you, I'm teaching an 11-year-old therapeutic foster girl how to express herself in writing a journal. She is a sexual abuse victim with ADHD, psychosis, epilepsy, and depression. She lives with me now. It's very hard at times managing her. She has schizophrenia and delusions. My prayer is that God heals her, and I want her to fulfill the purpose that God has for her. Aside from all that, I am still a full-time nurse at the same place and it's going okay. 'Melody' came to my office with something that happened Thursday. After checking her a couple times, we ended up basically kissing and making up as sister nurses. Love, Nicci XOXOXO

***

During the summer of June 2012, I took my career on a new escapade. I got a job as a travel nurse. I sold all my personal belongings and fit everything I had left into two suitcases. purchased a new 2012 Toyota Camry, and I started to my first assignment location. New Orleans, LA. I was only there for a couple months, but I jumped from facility to facility working, and I got to meet a lot of new people. One thing I learned was that every place had the same people and behaviors. They just had different faces. After New Orleans, I went to

California and after Cali, Hawaii. I worked in Hawaii the longest, and I loved it there. The weather, the diversity of culture, and the ocean. In all my life up until this point, I never dreamed that I would be doing this. I learned that whatever picture life paints as your beginning is not considered your destination point. Trusting God, obeying and listening to the Spirit within will take us to places we could never imagine.

CHAPTER SIX

A Mind Anew

As I looked over all my old journal entries, I saw how immature I was. I was broken. I didn't have any value in myself. And I let people steer me in any direction. I strongly disagree with the notion that a woman has the childhood dream of being promiscuous. I believe it results from a string of mismanaged decisions and negative influences. As women, we need to take a modified front and support one another with the awareness of our options, considering sexual expectations and practices. Abstinence and celibacy are a benefit to us, and it allows us to be free from emotional and mental clutter that can weigh down our spirits and prohibit spiritual growth.

The origin of a life of whoredoms can stem from a multitude of different reasons. Some may say daddy issues, molestations, hyper-sexed hormones, a generational curse also known as the Jezebel spirit, or even just being around others who practice a sexually lawless lifestyle. I believe mine came from molestations from people in my childhood. These experiences seem to have placed a stamp on my forehead that told others I was available. From the age of 6 to about 9, I engaged with older boys very inappropriately, and I'm embarrassed to admit that I even initiated the act at least half of the time to my recollection. (Though that is a normal response from an abused child.)

As victims of abuse, it's totally not our fault that this happened to us. But it is our absolute responsibility to get the counseling and healing that we need to lead emotionally successful and productive lives…not only for ourselves, but also for our families, partners and children. Broken people raise broken people, and I know you don't want to be the cause of another person's dysfunction.

By the time I went off to college, I had fallen for a guy that was part of the wrong crowd. That failed relationship left me heartbroken, and I began to engage sexually with men, and I became known as an easy girl with men. In this lifestyle, my feelings were numb, and I didn't care about most of the men I entertained, and I certainly could care less about my own self or well-being. I used them and looked at them as a financial gain instead of an opportunity for serious investment. I know I must have hurt a few of them that were genuinely interested in me. I know a couple of faces that come to mind now to whom I owe an apology. It was as if I dispatched myself to impersonal relations with them; my body was there, but my mind wasn't.

At the time, I didn't really stand for anything. Maybe I did, but I wasn't solid in my stand, so I fell for things. When a physical pass was made to me, I felt obligated in a way and would give in to the pressure. Another point I feel needs to be made regarding the matter is the education of our children. Both boys and girls. I don't recall ever having "the talk" with my parents while growing up. I understand all households are run differently, and the topic of sex in a conversation with your child is uncomfortable for some people. But consider the world telling and showing them what they need to know, or you are telling them. Never rob your daughters of the truth and make them fully aware of wolves in sheep's clothing.

Sometimes I think to myself if I had just listened to my intuition that God gave me, and had not always been second-guessing my gut feelings, I probably would have done better in the dating arena. On the other hand, as I look back, I could say that my promiscuous lifestyle wasn't my only issue. Along with the sexual activities came my being a traitor, deceitful, manipulative, and the list goes on and on. You see, bad spirits love company, and they just multiply by inviting all their friends. Not only was I loose, I had other bad fruit that I needed to deal with as well.

In God's Word, taken from Matthew 11:28, He says, *"Come unto me all ye who are weak and heavy laden, and I will give You rest."* I was spent; and by the time I became aware of my situation, I felt overwhelmed and didn't know where to start. That's when Jesus stepped in and my normal became uncomfortable. Unbeknownst to me, the season was changing and so was I.

* * *

I have found peace with my mother. I'll occasionally joke around with her and visit sometimes. The younger version of myself processed our relationship as me not being good enough, smart enough, funny enough, cool enough, pretty enough or talented enough for her attention and love. Ironically, I believed she found no value in me because there was none to be found.

The physical and emotional abandonment set a false standard in my mind that was etched there. A sick, twisted ideology I conjured up on how love was supposed to be and look like; Love was a confusing front, an emotional roller coaster full of tears and pain. I viewed love as inconsistent and untrustworthy. I witnessed early on in life that the root of betrayal was this crazy thing call Love. This toxic mindset spilled over into my romantic relationships. I allowed partners to be disrespectful and treat me poorly. I felt this was what I deserved, and I tolerated it from a broken place. Why, you ask? If I loved my mom and she loved me in return with her actions, then that is what this thing called love was. I am not going to place all the blame on my past relationships. Not only were my friends and lover's toxic, but I was also toxic too.

Until I felt the spirit leading me to isolate myself. I lost the desire of people to be close to. I began to lean into God more. At first, I thought I was going crazy. But crazy is a much better option than heart break. One can easily be happily crazy all day long but its impossible to be happily broken-hearted.

I started to feel another being inside my chest and core. It was inside of me, but it was separate from me, if that makes sense. It would roll around, flare up, get scared, and even giggle at times. A creature lived inside of me. It whispers, yells, talks softly, and even sings to me occasionally. I started listening to it. He has the power to comfort me. He is always so kind to me with his words. He says things to me that no one else has ever. He is so patient and encouraging. He taught me about myself. Taught me how to conduct myself around men and how to listen to his voice when he tells me to do something. He reminds me to think highly of myself and he compliments me when I am hard on myself.

I trust him completely and he has never gotten me into any trouble, if anything he gets me out of the trouble that I put myself in! He resides in our hiding place, my chest and core. He helped me to overcome anxiety and frustration. He hounded me into writing this book! One of the most prolific things he shared with me was about my mother. He told me that it's not that she does not love me, she cannot give me something that she doesn't have. I yearned for a greater love that she could not fill or even come close to. (Some of us are content with the love given to us my other humans. But there are some of us that have a deeper capacity for companionship and love on a whole different level and realm. No human can fill those places. Those places are intentionally placed there for the supernatural power of Christ. If we fail to fill that place with him; depression, feelings of emptiness, loneliness, and constant longing will always follow us.)

Some people have the gift of pouring, growing, and nurturing. My mom was not one of those persons. It's not that she did not see my value, she did not find any value in herself. Her treatment of me overall was an extension of how she felt about herself. It's kind of like a sickness, which lead to me having compassion for her and forgiveness.

In addition, drugs are demons from the inner most depths of hell. Not only did they wreak havoc on my childhood, but they have also repeated their encore millions of times to other children across the world. As hideous and wretched as they are; God's grace, love, and mercy is infinitely more surmounting than the beasts of drugs. His healing powers engulfed every avenue and hole in my body and spirit. In no way am I perfect and I do have my days like others. But on my worst day, I am nowhere close to what and who I use to be.

I enjoy my houseplants. Having a green thumb is something that is generational gifted to me from my father. In the past, I've had gardens where I've grown flowers, vegetables, and even fruits. But nothing comes close to the joy I get from keeping my houseplants. Waking up to their beauty and seeing them reside in corners of my little haven on earth allows me to be reminded of the goodness of God always. Over the years, through trial and error, I have learned things about them. I keep three different types of plants. First, are the vines. The nature of vines is eccentric. Vines are trainable, and they grow rather quickly with the proper environment. They can be trained to grow on walls, stakes, and even furniture if you allow them to. Their nature causes them to be somewhat aggressive at the same time. They will use their long arms and legs to wrap around other plants, and they can choke other houseplants out of sunlight and overtake them with the weight of their vines. Next, we have large-leafed foliage. I keep these because of their huge leaves and lovely appearance. Last, we have what I call the community shrubs. These plants feed off each other's hormones, and they thrive with some other species as neighbors. African violets are a good example.

Proper grooming of plants is important. As a keeper, trimming away dead leaves, rotating the plant, and proper watering is essential for them to thrive. Not all plants need to be watered at the same time. Some plants always require a dampened soil while others just need water once a month; and some need water only a few times a year. As a keeper, I understand this concept and I water my leafed pets when they need it. Depending upon a plant's native habitat, light requirements vary. Some plants can handle only low light levels because they naturally grow on the jungle floor where there isn't much light. If these low-light plants were to be placed in a bright area, they would instantly burn up because they are out of their usual position. Others need medium levels of light, while the majority really take off with full, direct sunlight. Some plants that require high light levels can be different colors other than the traditional green that we see them in.

As a keeper of houseplants, the key element to understand is a term called photosynthesis. Photosynthesis is the process by which green plants use sunlight to synthesize foods from carbon dioxide and water. Photosynthesis in plants generally involves the green pigment chlorophyll and generates oxygen as a byproduct.

God is our keeper. He is my keeper. When He found me, He had to trim away so-called friends, bad habits, a crippled mindset, and my lack of confidence and low self-esteem. I didn't have a keeper, or if I did, they weren't doing a good job at maintaining me. I was unidentifiable. God blew the breath of life on me and gave me His living water. He pruned my thinking and placed me in the shadows of low light so I could heal, rejuvenate, and grow. He rotates me so that I have balance and encourages my fruit to blossom. He placed me in an environment that was native to me. Peace, love, joy, well-rounded purity, and fellowship of other believers from whom I could feed. As women, understand that we need a keeper. Who is your keeper?

The enemy seeks to devour and destroy us. Always remember, he is a liar, and don't listen to his words:

* * *

I don't know how I got here. It wasn't sudden.

It creeped in little by little, 'til after a while it was full blown.

And now life is a struggle and colors are dull,

Life is empty and thankfulness has no meaning.

You're a liar.

It's binding my mind so I can't think straight.

Ties up my heart so I can't love and mutes my tongue so I can't articulate.

My need for help,

There is this constant hand around my throat.

I've been invaded;

You're a liar.

Reminding me of my past and robs my future.

Singing me lullabies of doom and gloom.

Tells me nobody has ever loved me and whispers that I'm damaged goods.

A parasite has encompassed my heart and is wrapped around my brain.

You're a liar.

The phone keeps ringing.

A harsh knocking keeps pounding at the door.

Nobody is there.

Trying to watch TV, things are jumping on me that I cannot see.

Insomnia is here and this mad voice repeatedly is calling my name.

Now, I'm sitting in this facility drugged out.

There it sits, at the end of my hospital bed,

Looking at me and me at it.

You're a liar.

Here, at my wit's end, but it lets up not. Continues to

Rip my confidence, self-esteem, faith, and worth from me.

Throwing it on a silver platter, with a sprinkle of my pride

As I watch the consumption of me.

It was eaten, and I was the audience,

Deforming my mind to a fetal position.

Yes, it snatched me off my high horse. But…

You're a liar.

I hear laughter in my agony;

In my silence, it found humor.

I've been defeated and now I await my death.

Shhh, Shhhh. What is that?

I hear something, I just felt something, innate

I found something

Hidden in the depths of my troubled mind.

I found a button. There's a warning on it;

It says: Caution. For Emergencies.

I pressed the button.

To hear these words…

My Dearly Beloved, I am with you

Even until the ends of the world.

Call upon Me and I will answer you.

Nicci, I see you and I have heard you.

I couldn't help you till you were on your back

To look at me. I want to show you how I

Specialize in the impossible. I love you and have

A big plan for you. I wanted you to experience

Rest, peace, happiness, joy, safety in Me.

I'm your best friend. You have finally found Me.

Here, in your heart. You had to go thru this to find Me.

You have now found your rightful position

With Me. Now, I want you to stand back and watch Me be God,

For there is no one else like Me. Be whole.

The words ended.

Something is happening, a gutting

I feel Him in my kneecaps.

I'm burning from the inside out.

What is this? That! What is this?

Oh, it's Deliverance!

I've heard of it before, but there is a difference

Between hearing it and feeling it, experiencing it

In my loins and piercing my soul.

Shhh shhhh, wait...

It's tingling my subconscious, running down my neck,

Rushing to my spinal cord;

I even feel You in my fingertips.

You're a liar.

There is something about the descendants of Adam,

You see, our creator instilled in us during our formation a chip.

I found this chip behind an impermeable wall

That only we have access to as createes during internal war.

When we press the button, it restarts our thought process,

Numbs old programming, scenarios and memories.

Even self-destructive behavior.

Depression, you're a liar.

Mania, you're a liar.

Schizophrenia, you're a liar.

Borderline Personality Disorder, you're a liar.

I see you looking at me.

I see you're in trouble.

Hey, press the button!!!

***

Inside, the club was loud. Music blared from the speakers and the DJ booth. The air was filled with cheap smoke and people. Having a drink and a no-named cigarette, she sat there to watch people. Suddenly, she got an eerie feeling. A strange feeling. Glancing at her hands, they were shaking, palms sweaty. GO HOME! an alarming voice commanded her. Flustered and scared, she jumped up and grabbed her purse before running to the car.

Nervously, she fumbled with keys to unlock the door. BAM! BAM! BAM! Shots fired off in the club. She could hear people screaming and running. All the while, the girl in the blue jacket sped off. While headed home, she was lost in her thoughts and asked herself," Who and what was that? God?" But why would He cover me like that? Me? In my filth? My wretchedness? That was Him. But why me? Why?"

A series of other events led her to a local church called New Life. She picked that church because its name connected with what she wanted…a new life, a new chance, a fresh start, a new beginning. The parking lot was jammed packed. So, she had to park way in the back. She didn't mind; when she exited the car, she could hear the saints worshipping—the musicians, and the choir. The sounds were electrifying, and it ignited a hope in her loins. Her spirit was excited, and she was anxious to sing along with the songs she remembered from her childhood. Once inside, she walked past 2 women at the door. They didn't speak, just looked her up and down. She was wearing a blue jacket.

Inside the sanctuary, she became uncomfortable. Looking for a seat, she spotted one. "Someone is sitting here." "This seat is taken!" The young woman nodded to the members that interrupted her trying to find somewhere to sit. Quickly, she began to look for another place. Paranoia started creeping in. She felt people staring at her. Discouraged and embarrassed, she spotted another space on a row with some kids. She quietly sat down, anticipating someone to excuse her again. But nobody did.

Look at me. Look at me. I was wearing a blue jacket. Do you remember me? I wanted acceptance. I was looking for confirmation. I wondered to myself if I was good enough to be there. Believe it or not, people in the nightclub were much friendlier than the people I encountered that day.

Our church growth is on life support. That empty seat next to you belongs to somebody. God is still calling people from darkness. How do you treat them when they get here? I didn't share this story for your pity or even attention. I shared it because I wanted you to know how it feels to be disappointed by people you would expect to be kind and warm. Or maybe you have forgotten what it felt like. That blue jacket carried shame, guilt and frustration.

Ephesians 4:2 reads, *"Be completely humble and gentle; be patient, bearing with one another in love."* Next time a stranger or even someone we see on a regular basis sits next to us, let's pour love, positivity and kindness into them. I'm reminding you to be disciples of Christ. You don't have to be an elder, pastor, usher or even a theology student.

Never forget this: Retention starts with you.

Are you ready for change? I remember several years ago; I was on a serious "hoe stroll." I'm ashamed to admit that I had sex with three different men in one weekend. After the escapades, I still was left empty, unsatisfied, and thinking of another person. I considered sex a sport, and I had a mentality of, "I'm a grown woman, and I need grown woman thangs!" I viewed men as conquests, and I liked the way they would respond to me when I made a pass at them. For some weird and demented reason, I thought that sleeping with them was like taking some of their strength. I looked at it as if I had won something.

And the pleasure I got out of being mean to them afterwards was rewarding. I had the upper hand, and I was able to initiate rejection.

I used men for sex and money. It stroked my ego. I saw myself as a playgirl and my friends were too. We would get together and share our conquests of how we played this dude or that guy, and we would sit back and laugh at their misfortune or their ignorance of our deceitful game. To add insult to injury, I was an intense party girl at the time; I smoked, was addicted to marijuana, and drank constantly. At the time I saw myself as living my best life and believed I was enjoying being single.

Little did I know, all those decisions were taking a toll on my psychological wellbeing. In all actuality, I was hurting. I used different men to replace the one that initially hurt me. All those negative emotions I had harvested into an anger, resentment and bitterness. I wanted to hurt them the way I had been hurt. I didn't want to become emotionally attached to someone, so I had several. Little did I know, I was a sad case. I was rotten on the inside. I kept a Journal of some of these things. Occasionally, I'll read through my old journals; clearly,

85% of my problems came from my choice of men and having inappropriate relations with them. I lacked boundaries.

A stirring began to take place on the inside once I became uncomfortable with myself on the outside; I was tired...tired of the games. I wanted what other women had but I believed I was damaged goods...too damaged for someone to feel special about me the way those other guys I would see seemed to feel about the women I saw them with. I wasn't good enough, and I didn't deserve it. My current lifestyle kept my mind's paradigm believing that I was lower than what I truly was. Which is a classic trick of the enemy. I wasn't too sure of how to go about changing it, but all I knew was that I was ready for a change. I wanted to be un-whored.

Internally, I was a mess. I always felt lonely and isolated. I was missing something. I was so lost and wrapped up in foolishness, that I didn't know whether I was coming or going. You see, God did not create women—or men—to have multiple partners. We were designed for one man or one woman; doing the opposite goes against our nature. Going against nature has serious repercussions and side effects. The effects I experienced was abnormalities in my relationships with people in general.

Over the years, research has been performed concerning the relationship between promiscuity and mental health issues. According to many of these scholarly articles, a link was found between sexual promiscuity and depression. According to professionals, casual sex is heavily linked to anxiety and depression. This was exactly what I was experiencing at the time. I wish I would have had someone to share these things with me. When we know better, we do better.

When I began my purity journey, my prayer life was key. After some time, my emotions gradually came back and I started to feel something that I hadn't felt before. Shame. I was ashamed of myself for multiple reasons. Along with the shame came a sense of unworthiness.

Through the Holy Spirit, Christ changed my thinking regarding men. The Spirit revealed to me that I was to look at them as my brothers and to view myself as their sister. In nature, siblings are of the same fold, and they help to protect each other. As women, we are our brothers' keeper, just as they are our keepers; and we need to have that view of them. Just as most of us have fathers, uncles, brothers, and male cousins, and in no way do we want someone to take advantage of them—we must treat other men the same way we would want our male family to be treated. God feels the same way about His children. Both men and women.

During a sermon, I heard about a loose woman in the Bible whom God used despite her past lifestyle. Let's dive into the story of Rahab from Joshua 2:1-24, KJV.

¹And Joshua the son of Nun sent out of Shittim two men to spy secretly, saying, Go view the land, even Jericho. And they went, and came into a harlot's house, named Rahab, and lodged there. ²And it was told the king of Jericho, saying, Behold, there came men in hither to night of the children of Israel to search out the country. ³And the king of Jericho sent unto Rahab, saying, bring forth the men that are come to thee, which are entered into thine house: for they be come to search out all the country. ⁴And the woman took the two men, and hid them, and said thus, There came men unto me, but I wist not whence they were: ⁵And it came to pass about the time of shutting of the gate, when it was dark, that the men went out: whither the men went I wot not: pursue after them quickly; for ye shall overtake them. ⁶But she had brought them up to the roof of the house, and hid them with the stalks of flax, which she had laid in order upon the roof. ⁷And the men pursued after them the way to Jordan unto the fords: and as soon as they which pursued after them were gone out, they shut the gate. ⁸And before they were laid down, she came up unto them upon the roof; ⁹And she said unto the men, I know that the LORD hath given you the end, and that your terror is fallen upon us, and that all the inhabitants of the land faint because of you. ¹⁰For we have heard how the LORD dried up the water of the Red sea for you, when ye came out of Egypt; and what ye did unto the two kings of the Amorites, that were on the other side Jordan, Sihon and Og, whom ye utterly destroyed. [11]And as soon as we had heard these things, our hearts did melt, neither did there remain any more courage in any man, because of you: for the LORD your God, he is God in heaven above, and in earth beneath. [12]Now therefore, I pray you, swear unto me by the LORD, since I have shewed you kindness, that ye will also shew kindness unto my father's house, and give me a true token: [13]And that ye will save alive my father, and my mother, and my brethren, and my sisters, and all that they have, and deliver our lives from death. [14]And the men answered her, our life for yours, if ye utter not this our business. And it shall be, when the LORD hath given us the land, that we will deal kindly and truly with thee. [15]Then she let them down by a cord through the window: for her house was upon the town wall, and she dwelt upon the wall. [16]And she said unto them, get you to the mountain, lest the pursuers meet you; and hide yourselves there three days, until the pursuers be returned: and afterward may ye go *your way. [17]And the men said unto her, we will be blameless of this thine oath which thou hast made us swear. [18]Behold, when we come into the land, thou shalt bind this line of scarlet thread in the window which thou didst let us down by: and thou shalt bring thy father, and thy mother, and thy brethren, and all thy father's household, home unto thee. [19]And it shall be, that whosoever shall go out of the doors of thy house into the street, his blood shall be upon his head, and we will be guiltless: and whosoever shall be with thee in the house, his blood shall be on our head, if any hand be upon him. [20]And if thou utter this our business, then we will be quit of thine oath which thou hast made us to swear. [21]And she said, according unto your words, so be it. And she sent them away, and they departed: and she bound the scarlet line in the window. [22]And they went, and came unto the mountain, and abode there three days, until the pursuers were returned: and the pursuers sought them throughout all the way but found them not. ²³So the two men returned, and descended from the mountain, and passed over, and came to Joshua the son of Nun, and told him all things that befell them: ²⁴And they said unto Joshua, Truly the LORD hath delivered into our hands all the land; for even all the inhabitants of the country do faint because of us.*

Rahab sensed there was something different about the spies. In her gut, she knew she wanted herself and her family to be a part of their mission. She heeded to the Spirit of God upon His prompting. The known prostitute was handpicked by God to be in on a big plan. She went on to marry Salmon of the tribe of Judah and produced a son by the name of Boaz. One of her great grandchildren's names was Jesse. Believe it or not, the Messiah came from her bloodline. Don't allow yourself to fall prey to negative thinking or consider yourself damaged goods. God has a plan for all of us, and if He redeemed Rahab's life, He can do the same for You.

Something that stuck in my mind was the question of what Rahab sensed in the spies. Was it a voice, a hunch, or just her trusting her woman's intuition? I'm left with answering my own question based on what I have personally experienced with God. Each of us has a piece of the Spirit that dwells within us. I am led to believe that Rahab was no different. A prompting in her thoughts concerning the spies led to her trust in them initially, following their Christ-like disposition; and in the end, they kept their word. With her heeding the Spirit of God, Rahab's household was spared. Consider your own life and the people with whom You engage—especially, but not limited to, men. Think about why you picked up this book. Are you ready for a change? Do you want to experience something different and start your new journey? Are you ready for a change?

CHAPTER SEVEN

Mindset of a Queen

C an I be honest? Do I have permission to be transparent and just be myself in this moment? I'm jealous...very jealous. Lord, please don't send me anyone because I don't know how to act. You see, if I am dating someone, I do not want that person to talk, look, think, or even smile at another female. I can't help it. Call me crazy. I know, I am a mess.

- It is cool, he has home girls. (twitch)

- His momma calls. (twitch) Whatever you got to say to him, you can say to me!

- He loves his dog named Daisy. (twitch)

- Oh, he's laughing at another girl's joke. (twitch)

- His sister is calling (twitch)

Even on the first date, I'd be thinking, "I'm not going to act crazy. I'm not going to act crazy." But after a while, it just slips out and Boom! I done went full-blown cray-cray. If he doesn't answer the phone on the first ring, I start talking to myself: "I will not drive over there. I will not jump the fence, wade through the bushes, I will not peer through his windows to see who he got over there! I'm not going to do it! Please don't let me get angry with this man."

Then I have to start talking to myself again! "I will not key his car or put a brick through his windshield! I'm not going to do it!"

That's why I'm still single! I can't get it right! By the way, this jealousy is set up. All the crazy girls say, "heeeeyyy!"

Call it insecurity, lack of confidence or low self-esteem; but the point-blank truth is that I am jealous, and I know it. Dudes have the nerve to complain about it. And my response would be, "Look, I like you and this is just a part of that. What do you want me to do? I'm a passionate person. Look, bruh, you can't pick which passion you want; either you take all of it or you take none of it."

I would wonder why the man I was interested in didn't get upset if my dad, brother or male friends called. Or why he didn't think of putting a tracker on my car? Finally, throughout my romantic relationships, I realized I was the only crazy one. My craziness was frowned upon by my partners and I was left emotionally lacking in return. I always felt lonely and isolated. I realized I needed an equal. I yearned for someone to match my intense energy. I wanted someone to be just as psycho for me as I was for them.

Loneliness. I was lonely.

Until one day

I met someone…

Wants me to talk to Him all day every day

Watches me when I sleep (twitch); He has superpowers.

He has a still, small voice that I can always barely hear.

Yes, and a familiar and kind voice.

Knows me better than I know myself.

I met someone…

Is constantly around and talks to me in my thoughts,

Encouraging me to open to Him and asks me what my hopes, dreams,

and aspirations are,

Gently guiding me step by step through growth, fears and do overs

I met someone…

He gave me the formula to freedom.

While everyone is asleep and while I am praying,

He tells me that a "suddenly" will be added to my prayers.

He then shakes up the equation and this produces a thing called

freedom.

I met someone…

I've never had anyone want to know me so intimately,

To care about my personal success,

Seeing my shortcomings and offering me a better way.

None of those other dudes could possibly come close to that.

I met someone…

Who loves me wholeheartedly,

And comes through for me consistently.

Who has never left or lied to me.

He told me that He formed me.

And the crazy girl within, He placed there, just for Him.

I met someone…

In order to change your life, you first need to come to the realization that an adjustment to your mindset is needed. This includes a new development in the way we make decisions in general. Decisions are based on what we know about the subject at the time the decision needs to be made or implemented. One attribute that I needed for myself was something called respect. Respect also goes hand in hand with finding value in ourselves—and value in our bodies and believing that they are something precious that does not call for us to treat them as a plaything like I was doing.

When I think of a Queen's mindset, I think of it as being distinguished, proud (in a good way) and strong. As a child, I wanted to be a princess. Now, as adult women, we have graduated to queens. As a young princess, I would play pretend in my imagination. I would change my attire to a fancy dress. I would walk, talk, and request things that I didn't have on a regular basis. In developing the mindset of a queen as an adult, I had to reconnect with the little girl that lives in all of us. But the first step I had to take was to acknowledge that I couldn't adjust my mindset single-handedly. I needed help.

We all need supernatural help from our creator. If you drove a Mercedes, would you take it to the Toyota dealership for maintenance? No, of course you wouldn't. You would take it to the Mercedes Benz dealership and have the mechanics there who specialize in your make and model perform the procedures needed because they are familiar with the vehicle. Well, the same thing applies for us.

I want you to stop and ask yourself, what is a Queen? What comes to your mind when you hear that word? Allow me to offer you a few definitions. First, a queen is the female ruler of an independent state, especially one who inherits the position by right of birth. Second, she is the most powerful chess piece that a chess player has, able to move any number of unobstructed squares in any direction along a rank, file, or diagonal on which she stands. As we think of a woman derived from royalty, we must ask ourselves what type of royalty do we descend from? The Royal priesthood, of course. We are all daughters of the Most High God, and we must assume our rightful position and conduct ourselves as such. Let's look at Queen Esther from the Bible. This Jewish orphan had a rag-to-riches story, so to speak. She was the second wife to King Xerxes, and we find her story in Esther 2:2-18:

> Then said the king's servants that ministered unto him, Let there be fair young virgins sought for the king: [3]And let the king appoint officers in all the provinces of his kingdom, that they may gather together all the fair young virgins unto Shushan the palace, to the house of the women, unto the custody of Hege the king's chamberlain, keeper of the women; and let their things for purification be given them: [4]And let the maiden which pleaseth the king be queen instead of Vashti. And the thing pleased the king; and he did so. [5]Now in Shushan the palace there was a certain Jew, whose name was Mordecai, the son of Jair, the son of Shimei, the son of Kish, a Benjamite; [6]Who had been carried away from Jerusalem with the captivity which had been

carried away with Jeconiah king of Judah, whom Nebuchadnezzar the king of Babylon had carried away. ⁷And he brought up Hadassah, that is, Esther, his uncle's daughter: for she had neither father nor mother, and the maid was fair and beautiful; whom Mordecai, when her father and mother were dead, took for his own daughter. ⁸So it came to pass, when the king's commandment and his decree was heard, and when many maidens were gathered together unto Shushan the palace, to the custody of Hegai, that Esther was brought also unto the king's house, to the custody of Hegai, keeper of the women. ⁹And the maiden pleased him, and she obtained kindness of him; and he speedily gave her things for purification, with such things as belonged to her, and seven maidens, which were met to be given her, out of the king's house: and he preferred her and her maids unto the best place of the house of the women. ¹⁰Esther had not shewed her people nor her kindred: for Mordecai had charged her

233

that she should not shew it. [11]And Mordecai walked every day before the court of the women's house, to know how Esther did, and what should become of her. [12]Now when every maid's turn was come to go in to king Ahasuerus, after that she had been twelve months, according to the manner of the women, (for so were the days of their purifications accomplished, to wit, six months with oil of myrrh, and six months with sweet odours, and with other things for the purifying of the women;) [13]Then thus came every maiden unto the king; whatsoever she desired was given her to go with her out of the house of the women unto the king's house. [14]In the evening she went, and on the morrow she returned into the second house of the women, to the custody of Shaashgaz, the king's chamberlain, which kept the concubines: she came in unto the king no more, except the king delighted in her, and that she were called by name. [15]Now when the turn of Esther, the daughter of Abihail the uncle of Mordecai, who had taken her for his daughter, was come to go in unto the king, she required nothing but what Hegai the king's chamberlain, the keeper of the women, appointed. And Esther obtained favour in the sight of all them that looked upon her. ¹⁶So Esther was taken unto king Ahasuerus into his house royal in the tenth month, which is the month Tebeth, in the seventh year of his reign. ¹⁷And the king loved Esther above all the women, and she obtained grace and favour in his sight more than all the virgins; so that he set the royal crown upon her head and made her queen instead of Vashti. ¹⁸Then the king made a great feast unto all his princes and his servants, even Esther's feast; and he made a release to the provinces, and gave gifts, according to the state of the king.

Why do You think the King chose Esther? I know why. It was for her killer shape; she had a body like Fort Knox and a sexy walk to go with it. I bet Esther had some mesmerizing selfies and her makeup was always slayed and flawless. No ma'am, it wasn't none of those things. Esther had a special spirit that illuminated her natural beauty.

* * * * *

The ancient question has burned in the hearts of many over the centuries:

What does God sound like?

Tell me! I want to know.

A man of God once stated that God sounds like, "A voice of rushing waters."

No, He sounds like thunder and lightning.

I got it, I got it. He sounds like the echoing heard on mountaintops.

His voice sounds as loud, crashing music with plenty of bass.

What does God sound like?

I don't know what He sounds like,

But I know what he feels like.

It's an instant warm feeling that slightly penetrates my heart and makes my face warm, flushed.

The cells in my body began to vibrate, spin and twirl in jubilee.

My respiratory system: inspiring and expiring becomes focused.

My integumentary system gooses up and

My digestive system turns and flips upside, downside, around side.

This body of mine is responding to the owner,

But what does He sound like?

I told You!

Start to tremble, and I can't feel my kneecaps, and my legs buckle and

My head is shaking.

But my heart, my heart has turned to jelly and is twisting clockwise,

leaping, pounding.

But what does He sound like?

My nervous system,

My chest has flamed, and my nerve endings have caught fire.

It's a body shake, innately

The atmosphere shifted and my homeostasis went supernatural.

There's a trembling in my carpals that I can't stop.

No, no, mo. I don't know what He sounds like.

But I know when He touches down

My internal thermometer freezes,

Insecurity disappears, depression runs,

Sadness melts, failures cease,

Psychosis flees, and my soul leaves the ICU.

My self-esteem gets off life support, and my confidence gets a whisper.

No, I don't know what He sounds like.

* * * * * * *

For us to be successful in this journey called life, we need to know what God sounds like or in my case, what he feels like. Especially in choosing our friends. Hearing from God for permission to accept certain people in our lives is a must. I have clearly given you some of my stories of so-called friends. But from those experiences, I've taken away a few lessons: I know when you hear the term "friends with benefits" we all think of a male friend that we allow ourselves to give sexual attention to. And since we are already on that subject, let's stay here awhile. I myself was guilty of the same thing, and I understand the concept completely—whether to meet physical needs or in the hope that the relationship will grow into something more.

If you have one or even multiple sex partners presently, start with verbalizing to them your desire to practice abstinence. Whatever their reaction is, don't allow any negativity or disapproval to take root in your thoughts or influence your decision on the matter. Remember that this is your life, and not theirs. Sexual purity is a road less traveled, and just because others don't choose it certainly does not mean that you can't. We have infinite power in words and speaking your desire for yourself means your words will be heard by you and by your spirit.

So, let the elimination process begin. Confess your sin of fornication to God and forsake it with His help. You need to stop the illicit sexual relations in your life, and here is why. The main reason for our celibacy or abstinence is to grow closer to God in every way possible. For this to happen, we need to glorify him with our bodies; and fornication is sin in God's eyes and nothing short of a distraction and a bondage we need to break. These sinful sexual favors we are giving to these men continue to allow soul ties to linger and prohibit our spiritual and mental growth. For biblical reference and example, please read John 8:1-11, KJV, below.

> *[1]Jesus went unto the mount of Olives. [2]And early in the morning he came again into the temple, and all the*

people came unto him; and he sat down and taught them. ³And the scribes and Pharisees brought unto him a woman taken in adultery; and when they had set her in the midst, ⁴They say unto him, Master, this woman was taken in adultery, in the very act. ⁵Now Moses in the law commanded us, that such should be stoned: but what sayest thou? ⁶This they said, tempting him, that they might have to accuse him. But Jesus stooped down, and with his finger wrote on the ground, as though he heard them not. ⁷So when they continued asking him, he lifted up himself, and said unto them, He that is without sin among you, let him first cast a stone at her. ⁸And again he stooped down and wrote on the ground. ⁹And they which heard it, being convicted by their own conscience, went out one by one, beginning at the eldest, even unto the last: and Jesus was left alone, and the woman standing in the midst. ¹⁰When Jesus had lifted up himself, and saw none but the woman, he said unto her, Woman, where are those thine accusers? hath no man condemned thee? [11]*She said, No man, Lord. And Jesus said unto her, neither do I condemn thee: go, and sin no more.*

The above unnamed adulteress had a soul-tie according to the text. Within one conversation, Christ severed her connection to these men, and she became whole at once. As single women of God, He wants us to Himself. He doesn't want to share us. The old Nicci had plenty of friends. I had friends that I called for different things, experiences or favors. My friends and I fed off each other and gave each other advice when problems arose. Their perspective was much like mine, and they groomed my way of thinking at the time towards scandal and prostituting the gifts that God gave me to serve Him. If I had kept them as friends, I would have remained the same. I needed some new friends to help me grow as the woman I was trying to become and the woman that He created me to be.

It's easy to hide yourself or someone else behind the title of "friend." In every relationship, there is a giver and a taker. Hopefully, each party participates from both sides. Even if there is a balance, does this friend contribute to what your goal is as woman/man of God? Is this person in the same mindset as you, or are they holding you back? Being attached, whether it be healthy or not, is a real issue that takes just as much effort to deal with as a romantic relationship.

Masturbation is another issue that hinders our relationship with God. Many don't fully understand the psychology behind it, and a full comprehension is needed. Look at masturbation as being a lover of yourself. You please yourself, and it glorifies nobody except you. While in the act of it, what type of thoughts run through your mind? Are they Christ-centered or smothered in sin? The verse that comes to mind is from Philippians 4:8, *"Finally, brothers and sisters, whatever is true, whatever is noble, whatever is right, whatever is pure, whatever is lovely, whatever is admirable—if anything is excellent or praiseworthy—think about such things."*

Let's chat about the commonly used term "best friend." Who is in your best friend position? Please don't think that I'm trying to talk you into breaking up with your bestie. I just want you to consider making God your bestie first.

The story of Ruth and Naomi has intrigued the minds of readers over the years, and I have heard dozens on sermons on these two women of God and their journey together as family, but mostly as friends. In Ruth 1:1-5, Naomi loses her husband and two sons. By the tenth verse, Naomi is preparing to go back home. Then, Naomi begins to argue with Ruth and Orpah (her two daughters-in-law) to leave her and return to their own people. Ruth 1:16-22, KJV, illustrates the deep connection and friendship between Ruth and Naomi.

Ruth replied to Naomi's urging by saying, *"Intreat me not to leave thee, or to return from following after thee: for whither thou goest, I will go; and where thou lodgest, I will lodge: thy people shall be my people, and thy God my God: Where thou diest, will I die, and there will I be buried: the Lord do so to me, and more also, if ought but death part thee and me."* When Naomi realized that Ruth was determined to go with her, she stopped urging her.

So, Ruth and Naomi traveled to Bethlehem. When they arrived, the whole town was stirred because of them, and the women exclaimed, "Can this be Naomi?"

"Don't call me Naomi," she told them. "Call me Mara, because the Almighty has made my life very bitter. I went away full, but the Lord has brought me back empty. Why call me Naomi? The Lord has afflicted me; the Almighty has brought misfortune upon me." So, Naomi returned from Moab accompanied by Ruth the Moabite, her daughter-in-law, arriving in Bethlehem as the barley harvest was beginning.

The rest of the story is history, literally. But this is the ideal friendship that God wants us to mirror in our daily lives with the people He places in our path. In no way are any of our relationships supposed to be exploited by the lust of our flesh or any type of manipulation.

CHAPTER EIGHT

Become Whole

I was a nurse for ten years before I began writing about my journey. In the nursing field, I had the opportunity to see and experience things that other professions couldn't offer. One of the toughest experiences I had to deal with while working geriatrics and hospice was dealing with death. It was emotionally taxing on me, and if I had developed a relationship with the family and patient, it made it extra hard because then I viewed the deceased as a distant relative. I remember one week when I had lost three of my favorite patients. Talk about a hard blow. I ended up in my boss's office ready to quit, and she encouraged me to continue being a nurse for the same reason I became one. I became desensitized to a lot of things, but death was never one of them. I always had the same emotion with each patients' death, grief and a great sense of loss. It was a natural part of life, however, and I was left with the feeling that I had at least been able to contribute something positive to their lives before they passed.

In hindsight, there is another form of death that I experienced while in college. Many years before my nursing life, it all began with a party friend I'll call Wanda. I clearly remember one evening she had called while I was at home drinking and getting high with another friend. She sounded different and a little scared. She told me she was pregnant by one of her random dudes and asked me what I wound do in that position. Out of obvious ignorance and under the influence, I told her that I would get rid of it; I went on to tell her that we didn't have time to be tied down to a crying baby. She then asked me if I wound go with her to the clinic the following day at 2 pm, and I agreed.

Pulling into the parking lot was uneventful, and I viewed this appointment like any other doctor visit. What was about to happen didn't sink in until I stepped foot into the lobby of the clinic. The atmosphere was cold and emotionally crippling; suddenly I was paralyzed with fear. You might wonder what scared me the most? It was the faces of the women that were there. None of them were nonchalant. They were there due to bad circumstances, not because they didn't want the babies—at least, that is how it seemed to me. I'll never forget this couple that sat across from us. The woman kept rubbing her abdomen and then leaning on the guy she was with. His facial expression didn't exhibit an ounce of remorse or care, and he would gently pull his shoulder from her head. They continued this until she was called back. As the door opened to the back, I saw the young doctor in a white coat sitting on a stool or some steps. His countenance was that of circumstance as well in my opinion. Everything was so quiet, you could have heard a pin drop. The first woman I witnessed come from the back was young; she had great skin and long black hair—but I'll NEVER forget her face. I saw shock, as though she had seen a ghost, and I saw emptiness. She looked lost. She looked half dead to me. It was as if she was missing a part of herself. She, too, was holding her abdomen. The friend who had accompanied her took her from the nurse and assisted her to the exit. Through the window I watched them pull away.

As for Wanda, I don't know what or how she was processing our surroundings, but I was nervous for her and got cold feet. I wanted to leave, and I felt as though this place was haunted. It scared me, but I was frozen. I couldn't move or even say anything to her. I wanted to tell her that we should go now, but I didn't have control over my body. The nurse called her name, and she got up and went to the back. My heart started racing, my gums were throbbing, I was sweating, and my hands were shaking. I could feel my nose tingling, and I wanted to cry. I don't recall how long she was back there, but I remember the nurse coming out and Wanda looking for me to help her to the car as she too held her abdomen. I stared at both for a long time until I heard the receptionist ask me if I was okay. I snapped out of it and went to place my arm around Wanda. As we were exiting the lobby, she whispered something to me that I will never forget: "Don't ever do this, Nicci, it's the worst feeling in the world." Goosebumps came on my skin, and we left. She spent the next couple days on meds, resting at my apartment.

As a nurse, I witnessed the death of adults. It was easier to process their deaths because in general they had experienced childhood and life. In no way am I trying to sound insensitive, but death that comes with the spirit of abortion is like no other, and I wouldn't wish it on my worst enemy.

As I think back to this experience, I see myself just as guilty as Wanda, her random dude, the nurse, and the doctor. Since then, I have asked God for forgiveness in aiding in the death of one of His creations, and He has forgiven me. I tell you this story to remind you of one of the potential results of not practicing abstinence. No, not all unmarried women have abortions, but some feel they must and do. I want to spare you from the hurt, pain and resentment that comes along with this act. I'd rather you experience abortion through my story rather than personally. But if this story is already a part of your story, I want you to give that child a name. I want you to ask God for healing; realize that He can make you whole, even after an abortion. All of us have fallen short of the glory of God, and He continues to love us unconditionally.

Not only do we want to become sexually abstinent, but we want to be made whole; this is the finished product we are aiming for. This process will probably take the longest and requires the most consistent prayer. If you're intimidated by the concept of prayer, don't be. God isn't looking for you to be long, drawn-out, articulate, or even eloquent in what you say to him. He just wants you to be honest and transparent. Think of how raw you are with your close friend. God desires that same energy, but with more intimacy. Just talk to Him. Mainly, pray for emotional healing. Back some time ago, I needed healing from the childhood trauma of a parental figure's behavior that constantly disappointed and rejected me. I needed healing from past romantic relationships in which I experienced betrayal, and I needed to heal my mind so I could cease my self-destructive behaviors. Being fully content with our life and position is necessary for our inner peace.

Proverbs 24:3 cautions us to guard our hearts. This can mean many things and is interpreted to convey different messages. As a woman wanting wholeness, protecting the avenues into our lives is required. Engaging in premarital sex is considered an avenue into the heart. In no way am I saying that sex is bad. What I am saying is that unsanctified sex is sinful and has subconscious side effects. During our journey as women of God, we strive for righteousness—righteousness in our thoughts, behaviors, decisions and relationships.

I want to challenge you to do something for 30 days. Girl do not get all stressed out. If you can do the 30-day squat challenge for a bigger bum, the 30-day oil your scalp challenge for hair growth, and the 30-day challenge of drink one gallon of water daily for clearer skin, then you can do this. For 30 days, I want you to pray three times a day. That's it. Pray upon rising, at lunch, and before going to bed. During these prayer times, I want you to focus on what bothers you the most. Focus on what you have hidden and buried within your thoughts. We want to start our healing from the inside out.

While we are focusing on God and His work that He wants to accomplish through us, that annoying emotional connection to past trauma is severed. It's a phenomenon referred to as a transfer of power. Let me try to break this down. You see, operating in the power of the Holy Spirit releases supernatural power. And while we are busy working, that heavenly power infiltrates the crevasses of our mind and heals us inside. Broken things are mended by this power. It's crazy, but I've experienced it firsthand and it's a hundred percent true. If you don't believe me, just try it.

God specializes in the impossible. He is the God of the impossible. Look at Luke 13:10-12, KJV:

> *And he was teaching in one of the synagogues on the sabbath. And behold, there was a woman who had a spirit of infirmity eighteen years, and was bowed together, and could in no wise lift up herself. And when Jesus saw her, he called her to him, and said unto her, Woman, thou art loosed from thine infirmity.*

What this woman needed was freedom from her infirmity. Wholeness and freedom go hand in hand. In freedom, wholeness arrives. Acts 16:16-40 tells a story of two men, Paul and Silas. These innocent men were beaten and jailed for sharing the gospel and healing the sick. While tied in shackles, at midnight these great men of faith began praying and singing hymns to God. Their audience were other prisoners. An earthquake shook the prison, and their ties were loosened, and the doors of the prison flung open. Upon their departure from the prison, they ministered to a prison guard and other prisoners.

Most of us don't even realize we are in shackles. We don't know that we are in bondage because we have been in it so long, we don't know what true freedom feels or tastes like. Think about what you're tied up with. It might not be shackles or confinement to a prison, but it may be sickness or ailment. Maybe even a relationship or trying to keep up with other people. What has you bound? Drugs? Alcohol? Financial bondage? Or like I was, perhaps you're bound to a negative view of yourself. Whatever it is, I want to offer you the formula to freedom that produces wholeness.

Consider the story of Paul and Silas. I'm in no way a mathematician, but I converted their freedom into a formula. Like, a+b=c. Praying at midnight, in the wee hours of the morning is (a); God adding a shaking is (b). Your earnest prayers (a) plus God's shaking (b) equals freedom (c) as the product. If by chance, the shaking doesn't arrive, continue praying until the shaking arrives. In order to experience something that you never had; you are going to have to do something that you have never done.

Think about society's definition of a 'real' woman: her hair is on point, her nails are done, her outfits are fly, she smells good, she has an education, a job, and a house. And this is all true to some extent. However, let's dig a little deeper into the actual characteristics of a woman of God. I don't want to sound like a pastor but, let's examine Proverbs 31:10-31.

10Who can find a virtuous woman? for her price is far above rubies. 11The heart of her husband doth safely trust in her, so that he shall have no need of spoil. 12She will do him good and not evil all the days of her life. 13She seeketh wool, and flax, and worketh willingly with her hands. 14She is like the merchants' ships; she bringeth her food from afar. 15She riseth also while it is yet night, and giveth meat to her household, and a portion to her maidens. 16She considereth a field, and buyeth it: with the fruit of her hands she planteth a vineyard. 17She girdeth her loins with strength, and strengtheneth her arms. 18She perceiveth that her merchandise is good: her candle goeth not out by night.

[19]She layeth her hands to the spindle, and her hands hold the distaff. [20]She stretcheth out her hand to the poor; yea, she reacheth forth her hands to the needy. [21]She is not afraid of the snow for her household: for all her household are clothed with scarlet. [22]She maketh herself coverings of tapestry; her clothing is silk and purple. [23]Her husband is known in the gates, when he sitteth among the elders of the land. [24]She maketh fine linen, and selleth it; and delivereth girdles unto the merchant. [25]Strength and honour are her clothing; and she shall rejoice in time to come. [26]She openeth her mouth with wisdom; and in her tongue is the law of kindness. [27]She looketh well to the ways of her household, and eateth not the bread of idleness. [28]Her children arise up, and call her blessed; her husband also, and he praiseth her. [29]Many daughters have done virtuously, but thou excellest them all. [30]Favour is deceitful, and beauty is vain: but a woman that feareth the LORD, she shall be praised. [31]Give her of the fruit of

her hands; and let her own works praise her in the gates.

This rare breed of woman is many things, but a whore she is not. She is trustworthy, productive, and business-minded; she masters multi-tasking, she invests her money, is kind to the indigent, displays a good work ethic, is creative, and doesn't embrace fear on any level. She is also well respected for her work and, above all these, she loves the Lord and holds Him in high esteem.

We read a story in the Bible about another woman of God named Dorcas, also known as Tabitha. We find her story in Acts 9:36-42.

[36]Now there was at Joppa a certain disciple named Tabitha, which by interpretation is called Dorcas: this woman was full of good works and almsdeeds which she did. [37]And it came to pass in those days, that she was sick, and died: whom when they had washed, they laid her in an upper chamber. [38]And forasmuch as Lydda was nigh to Joppa, and the disciples had heard that Peter was there, they sent unto him two men,

desiring him that he would not delay to come to them.
[39]Then Peter arose and went with them. When he was
come, they brought him into the upper chamber: and all
the widows stood by him weeping, and shewing the
coats and garments which Dorcas made, while she was
with them. [40]But Peter put them all forth, and kneeled
down, and prayed; and turning him to the body said,
Tabitha, arise. And she opened her eyes: and when she
saw Peter, she sat up. [41]And he gave her his hand, and
lifted her up, and when he had called the saints and
widows, presented her alive. [42]And it was known
throughout all Joppa; and many believed in the Lord.

Tabitha was a woman of high integrity and her fruit would speak of her high-quality characteristics. The Bible does not say a whole lot about Tabitha's prayer life but based on this simple excerpt of her life and position, I can guarantee you she had a phenomenal prayer life. Tabitha had a certain spirit upon her. She attracted people with her gift of the spirit. She was living within her purpose, and she was successfully achieving the assignments the Lord had given to her.

Her spirit with God and her purpose were so much in alignment with Christ that, upon her untimely death, God gave resurrection power to Peter to bring her back to life to finish her duties and to live out a testament of the will of God.

Another great woman was Abigail. Her story is found in 1 Samuel 25:1-42.

> *¹And Samuel died; and all the Israelites were gathered together, and lamented him, and buried him in his house at Ramah. And David arose, and went down to the wilderness of Paran. ²And there was a man in Maon, whose possessions were in Carmel; and the man was very great, and he had three thousand sheep, and a thousand goats: and he was shearing his sheep in Carmel. ³Now the name of the man was Nabal; and the name of his wife Abigail: and she was a woman of good understanding, and of a beautiful countenance: but the man was churlish and evil in his doings; and he was of the house of Caleb. ⁴And David heard in the wilderness that Nabal did shear his sheep. ⁵And David sent out ten*

young men, and David said unto the young men, Get

you up to Carmel, and go to Nabal, and greet him in my

name: ⁶And thus shall ye say to him that liveth in

prosperity, Peace be both to thee, and peace be to thine

house, and peace be unto all that thou hast. ⁷And now I

have heard that thou hast shearers: now thy shepherds

which were with us, we hurt them not, neither was there

ought missing unto them, all the while they were in

Carmel. ⁸Ask thy young men, and they will shew thee.

Wherefore let the young men find favour in thine eyes:

for we come in a good day: give, I pray thee,

whatsoever cometh to thine hand unto thy servants, and

to thy son David. ⁹And when David's young men came,

they spake to Nabal according to all those words in the

name of David, and ceased. ¹⁰And Nabal answered

David's servants, and said, Who is David? and who is

the son of Jesse? there be many servants now a days

that break away every man from his master. ¹¹Shall I

then take my bread, and my water, and my flesh that I

have killed for my shearers, and give it unto men, whom I know not whence they be? ¹²So David's young men turned their way, and went again, and came and told him all those sayings. ¹³And David said unto his men, Gird ye on every man his sword. And they girded on every man his sword; and David also girded on his sword: and there went up after David about four hundred men; and two hundred abode by the stuff. ¹⁴But one of the young men told Abigail, Nabal's wife, saying, Behold, David sent messengers out of the wilderness to salute our master; and he railed on them. ¹⁵But the men were very good unto us, and we were not hurt, neither missed we any thing, as long as we were conversant with them, when we were in the fields: ¹⁶They were a wall unto us both by night and day, all the while we were with them keeping the sheep. ¹⁷Now therefore know and consider what thou wilt do; for evil is determined against our master, and against all his household: for he is such a son of Belial, that a man cannot speak to him. [18]Then Abigail made haste, and took two hundred loaves, and two bottles of wine, and five sheep ready dressed, and five measures of parched corn, and an hundred clusters of raisins, and two hundred cakes of figs, and laid them on asses. [19]And she said unto her servants, Go on before me; behold, I come after you. But she told not her husband Nabal. [20]And it was so, as she rode on the ass, that she came down by the covert on the hill, and, behold, David and his men came down against her; and she met them. [21]Now David had said, Surely in vain have I kept all that this fellow hath in the wilderness, so that nothing was missed of all that pertained unto him: and he hath requited me evil for good. [22]So and more also do God unto the enemies of David, if I leave of all that pertain to him by the morning light any that pisseth against the wall. [23]And when Abigail saw David, she hasted, and lighted off the ass, and fell before David on her face, and bowed herself to the ground, [24]And fell at his feet, and said, Upon me, my lord, upon me let this iniquity be: and let thine handmaid, I pray thee, speak in thine audience, and hear the words of thine handmaid. ²⁵Let not my lord, I pray thee, regard this man of Belial, even Nabal: for as his name is, so is he; Nabal is his name, and folly is with him: but I thine handmaid saw not the young men of my lord, whom thou didst send. ²⁶Now therefore, my lord, as the LORD liveth, and as thy soul liveth, seeing the LORD hath withholden thee from coming to shed blood, and from avenging thyself with thine own hand, now let thine enemies, and they that seek evil to my lord, be as Nabal. ²⁷And now this blessing which thine handmaid hath brought unto my lord, let it even be given unto the young men that follow my lord. ²⁸I pray thee, forgive the trespass of thine handmaid: for the LORD will certainly make my lord a sure house; because my lord fighteth the battles of the LORD, and evil hath not been found in thee all thy days. ²⁹Yet a man is risen to pursue thee, and to seek thy soul: but the soul of my lord shall be bound in the bundle of life with the LORD thy God; and the souls of thine enemies, them shall he sling out, as out of the middle of a sling. ³⁰And it shall come to pass, when the LORD shall have done to my lord according to all the good that he hath spoken concerning thee, and shall have appointed thee ruler over Israel; ³¹ That this shall be no grief unto thee, nor offence of heart unto my lord, either that thou hast shed blood causeless, or that my lord hath avenged himself: but when the LORD shall have dealt well with my lord, then remember thine handmaid. ³²And David said to Abigail, Blessed be the LORD God of Israel, which sent thee this day to meet me: ³³And blessed be thy advice, and blessed be thou, which hast kept me this day from coming to shed blood, and from avenging myself with mine own hand. ³⁴For in very deed, as the LORD God of Israel liveth, which hath kept me back from hurting thee, except thou hadst hasted and come to meet me, surely there had not been left unto Nabal by the morning light any that pisseth against the wall. ³⁵So David received of her hand that which she had brought him, and said unto her, Go up in peace to thine house; see, I have hearkened to thy voice, and have accepted thy person. ³⁶And Abigail came to Nabal; and, behold, he held a feast in his house, like the feast of a king; and Nabal's heart was merry within him, for he was very drunken: wherefore she told him nothing, less or more, until the morning light. ³⁷But it came to pass in the morning, when the wine was gone out of Nabal, and his wife had told him these things, that his heart died within him, and he became as a stone. ³⁸And it came to pass about ten days after, that the LORD smote Nabal, that he died. ³⁹And when David heard that Nabal was dead, he said, Blessed be the LORD, that hath pleaded the cause of my reproach from the hand of Nabal, and hath kept his servant from evil: for the LORD hath returned the wickedness of Nabal upon his own head. And David sent and communed with Abigail, to take her to him to wife. ⁴⁰And when the servants of David were come to Abigail to Carmel, they spake unto her, saying, David sent us unto thee, to take thee to him to wife. ⁴¹And she arose, and bowed herself on her face to the earth, and said, Behold, let thine handmaid be a servant to wash the feet of the servants of my lord. ⁴²And Abigail hasted, and arose and rode upon an ass, with five damsels of hers that went after her; and she went after the messengers of David, and became his wife.

As women, our strength is in our hands and hearts. Allowing society to dictate to our femininity and segregating our value to our ability to have sex is a repugnant use of the glory with which God has blessed us with. The world is not going to tell us where our power is hidden. But God has given us admirable women in the Bible as examples that we can mirror and reflect on.

CHAPTER NINE

Confidence Boosters

While battling depression, I didn't care too much about the clothes I wore. If they were clean, fit, and didn't have holes in them, I was pretty much content. Sometimes, my friends would make small comments about how I dressed, but I would just dismiss their suggestions. I didn't realize at the time how much of a billboard we are to the world. What we wear and how we wear it tells others our story, how we feel about ourselves, and even where we are in life.

Taking the necessary time to take care of our personal appearance gets the attention of others. Not that we live to please others, but we want and need to dress to impress. We all want people to respect us and treat us with dignity. Paying closer attention to our aesthetics as women increases our chances of achieving what we desire in the areas of friendships, employment and even finances. When we look good, we attract good.

Equally important, always add a smile to every outfit of the day. Smiling at strangers is therapeutic for them and us. A smile also pours into people; it is a kinder form of service that requires little effort. Keep in mind that service to others is the key to our own happiness. During your prayers, ask God to open your heart so you can connect with people spiritually. The simple gesture of smiling is food to a weary soul. Trust me, I know how it feels to be on the receiving end of a warm smile on a hard day.

Our physical health is extremely important to our confidence and detrimental to our bodies when we ignore it; keeping yourself in tip-top shape is not only boosts our confidence, but also enhances our overall health. Keeping our body fat percentage within a healthy range greatly decreases our chances of contracting many different illnesses that people are more susceptible to because of poor diet and obesity.

A negative stigma surrounds mental health; people are reluctant to be transparent about where their mind is and whether they are in a healthy mental space or not. Counseling does have intense work attached to it, but whatever you put in, you will get back—at least, that has been true for me. How we view ourselves in our mind is how we will allow others to treat us. Mental clarity and healing should be a priority for us all. Good mental space is a foundational block that we need as women to be successful.

Where are you spiritually? I'm not asking what church you belong to nor am I asking what religion or denomination you identify with. I'm asking where you stand with God, and are you embracing Him as much as you embrace your job, education, family, friends, etc.

One thing that took me years to develop was emotional stability. At times, I would allow others' actions, words and behavior to dictate how I felt, what I did, and how I valued myself. Being emotionally sound as a woman is liberating, and it is totally necessary in order to complete our confidence training. To be honest, I found emotionally stability in my prayer life, and it then spilled over into my day-to-day activities. Every time I got emotional (confused, jealous, fearful, or even tempted), I would instantly pray. If I was at work, I would go to the bathroom. If I was at home, I would go to my room and hit the floor, face down. If I was in a store, I'd start whispering a prayer under my breath. I would tell God what just happened to initiate the strong emotion. Then, I would tell Him how it was currently making me feel and what I wanted to do about it in my flesh. Afterwards, I would ask Him what I should do. Then I'd ask Him to shift my attitude and take away those negative feelings. I'm not going to lie; it took a few months for my mind to adapt to this thinking, but I became solid. As women, we are sensitive and emotional. But we must manage those gifts, so they are productive to us. We must oversee them, so that they are not in charge of us.

Take a closer look at your relationships—include the ones that aren't romantic. I'm speaking of all of them in general. Are your relationships solid? It is impossible to have confidence in a shaky foundation. Make sure the core people in your life are dependable and you have positive experiences with them. We all know nobody is perfect, but what is the energy of the people with whom you interact? Think about it; it may require you to take an inventory of your life and decide who can stay and who gets the boot. It's your life; you are in control and removing negative people is necessary for personal growth at times.

Next, we have purpose. What is your purpose? Every woman has a purpose; God has given all of us purpose. Discover your purpose. You'll find that your purpose is hidden behind your passion. Let's explore the story of Hannah taken from 1 Samuel 1:1-28, KJV:

> *¹Now there was a certain man of Ramathaimzophim, of mount Ephraim, and his name was Elkanah, the son of Jeroham, the son of Elihu, the son of Tohu, the son of Zuph, an Ephrathite: ²And he had two wives; the name of the one was Hannah, and the name of the other Peninnah: and Peninnah had children, but Hannah had no children. ³And this man went up out of his city yearly to worship and to sacrifice unto the LORD of hosts in Shiloh. And the two sons of Eli, Hophni and Phinehas, the priests of the LORD, were there. ⁴And when the time was that Elkanah offered, he gave to Peninnah his wife, and to all her sons and her daughters, portions: ⁵But unto Hannah he gave a worthy portion; for he loved*

Hannah: but the LORD had shut up her womb. ⁶And her adversary also provoked her sore, for to make her fret, because the LORD had shut up her womb. ⁷And as he did so year by year, when she went up to the house of the LORD, so she provoked her; therefore she wept, and did not eat. ⁸Then said Elkanah her husband to her, Hannah, why weepest thou? and why eatest thou not? and why is thy heart grieved? am not I better to thee than ten sons? ⁹So Hannah rose up after they had eaten in Shiloh, and after they had drunk. Now Eli the priest sat upon a seat by a post of the temple of the LORD. ¹⁰And she was in bitterness of soul, and prayed unto the LORD, and wept sore. ¹¹And she vowed a vow, and said, O LORD of hosts, if thou wilt indeed look on the affliction of thine handmaid, and remember me, and not forget thine handmaid, but wilt give unto thine handmaid a man child, then I will give him unto the LORD all the days of his life, and there shall no razor come upon his head. ¹²And it came to pass, as she continued praying before the LORD, that Eli marked her mouth. [13]Now Hannah, she spake in her heart; only her lips moved, but her voice was not heard: therefore Eli thought she had been drunken. [14]And Eli said unto her, How long wilt thou be drunken? put away thy wine from thee. [15]And Hannah answered and said, No, my lord, I am a woman of a sorrowful spirit: I have drunk neither wine nor strong drink but have poured out my soul before the LORD. [16]Count not thine handmaid for a daughter of Belial: for out of the abundance of my complaint and grief have I spoken hitherto. [17]Then Eli answered and said, go in peace: and the God of Israel grant thee thy petition that thou hast asked of him. [18]And she said, let thine handmaid find grace in thy sight. So, the woman went her way, and did eat, and her countenance was no more sad. [19]And they rose up in the morning early, and worshipped before the LORD, and returned, and came to their house to Ramah: and Elkanah knew Hannah his wife; and the LORD remembered her. ²⁰*Wherefore it came to pass, when the time was come about after Hannah had conceived, that she bare a son, and called his name Samuel, saying, Because I have asked him of the LORD.* ²¹*And the man Elkanah, and all his house, went up to offer unto the LORD the yearly sacrifice, and his vow.* ²²*But Hannah went not up; for she said unto her husband, I will not go up until the child be weaned, and then I will bring him, that he may appear before the LORD, and there abide for ever.* ²³*And Elkanah her husband said unto her, Do what seemeth thee good; tarry until thou have weaned him; only the LORD establish his word. So the woman abode, and gave her son suck until she weaned him.* ²⁴*And when she had weaned him, she took him up with her, with three bullocks, and one ephah of flour, and a bottle of wine, and brought him unto the house of the LORD in Shiloh: and the child was young.* ²⁵*And they slew a bullock, and brought the child to Eli.* ²⁶*And she said,*

Oh my lord, as thy soul liveth, my lord, I am the woman that stood by thee here, praying unto the LORD. [27]For this child I prayed; and the LORD hath given me my petition which I asked of him: [28]Therefore also I have lent him to the LORD; as long as he liveth he shall be lent to the LORD. And he worshipped the LORD there.

Peniniah   was Hannah's adversary, and she provoked a sore spot that developed into depression. As we are aware, in those days and still today in our society and others around the world, a barren woman carries a stigma. Hannah became depressed and felt as if she had no value. She lacked confidence in herself, her marriage and her position in her community. Her distress led to her total surrender to God and she made a solemn promise to Him. God, in turn, granted her request; but the request she made was in His hands, and she was chosen to be Samuel's mother way before Hannah was even born and before the presence of Peninah. With her promised child, Hannah found her confidence through fulfilling the purpose in God, and when she completed her assignment, He gave her more children.

Our stories may not be the exact same as Hannah's, but we can draw from her experience that faith in God, us keeping our promises to Him, and being obedient to His will produces our confidence.

Once you have begun your abstinence journey, the coast will not be clear, and temptations lurk at every available opportunity. Just focus on the friendship aspect when it comes to men and dating. Please, know you are human. Even people who have chosen a life of celibacy still get tempted. It's how you deal with the temptation, but more importantly how you avoid it. To be honest, I'm a very touchy-feely person—especially with a handsome guy. I'm aware of this, and with God as my conscience, I purposely maintain a healthy distance physically with men that I date or have as friends. Practicing good, healthy boundaries is very beneficial to your success as an abstinent woman when you're not in a marriage relationship.

Another important factor is to let your gentlemen friends know exactly where you stand on the matter. You don't have to send out a memo before the first date, but you do need to mention it if it comes up or he hints about it. Some men test the waters to observe your reaction. Stand firm in your position, and if they continue to ask you about changing your mind or compromising for them, dismiss them from your life respectfully. We need friends who honor our commitment to Christ, be they man or woman; if they can't, we certainly don't need them in our lives. 1 Corinthians 6:19-20 states, *"Do you not know that your bodies are the temple of the Holy Spirit, who is in You, whom You have received from God? You are not your own. You were bought at a price. Therefore, honor God with your bodies."*

Other practices can aid you in maintaining morally correct behavior with men, First, do not allow sexual topics and preferences to drift into your conversations. Most actions began with thoughts, thought become words, and words are followed by actions. Eliminate all the possibilities; don't hang out at night alone by yourselves. Do group outings or double dates to be eliminate temptation. Also, choose friends who have the same values you do or that you wish to have. Take note of the old saying, "Bad company corrupts good morals."

Please believe that your youth is the most special time of your live, and who we give this precious time to is a decision that requires supernatural wisdom. When we sexually engage with someone, we create a soul tie. Sex is a glue that merges two people together, whether with one partner or many. A piece of our sexual partners is bound to us for the rest of our lives. During an abstinence journey, with prayer and strength from God, soul-ties can be broken. Abstinence will change who you are—you will no longer identify as a whore—and give you a remarkable experience. This change for the better will undoubtedly spill over into other areas of your life.

I am an avid coffee drinker, and it is a part of my morning routine. I prepare my coffee the same way every day, and it never fails to get me going. While living in Hawaii, I experienced real, authentic Kona coffee. Kona coffee is highly prized throughout the world and the actual tree thrives on Hawaii's rich, volcanic soil. The actual bean itself has a full-bodied flavor and a pleasing aroma. This coffee is grown in only one area of the world, and the Kona coffee farmer is highly respected.

I was grateful to have had the opportunity to tour a coffee farm. During this tour, I learned a great deal about the popular morning beverage. The coffee tree takes, on average, three to four years to produce a favorable crop. The bean can be harvested in three different stages, and each stage has a different taste. The coffee cherry, the green bean, and the fully roasted stage. Did I mention that the beans are hand-picked?

During the tree's maturating phase, it's very susceptible to succumbing to failure. A young tree must be protected from the elements. The farmer must provide an adequate irrigation system to supply the proper amount of water. Netting protects the young trees from flying pests that may cause harm. I also observed support stakes in the ground next to the young trees, and wire was used to support the tree to keep it upright and prevent it from leaning.

Once it is mature, the tree can filter its own water and stand against the birds. The trunk is more solid, and the heavy winds can't knock it down. The wise farmer has aided in establishing a firm foundation for the roots until the tree develops its own strength. If it weren't for the farmer spending the time to invest in his crop, he wouldn't get the benefits of the fruit (and neither would we). The farmer has value in his plants and while they are still seedlings, he knows of their potential and how to care for them. In return, others find value in his finished product. Just as the farmer sees the value in his precious coffee trees, even when they are young and unable to take care of themselves—Christ has infinite love for us and helps to mature and developed the strength we need to stand.

Every girl I know has dreams of a huge wedding. Most of them dream of beautiful flowers, family, friends, presents, a designer dress, amazing hair, and great pictures to spend a lifetime reminiscing over. But marriage is more than the wedding and the pictures—it is a serious commitment. Before we entertain the idea of picking a lifetime mate, we need to consider how the union will glorify God. To glorify God, we must select our future mate with His guidance. It doesn't matter what your social circle thinks of your choice. First, we need to ask God. And after seeking His answer, we must ultimately respect His response. Ignoring what He has said to us regarding the person we fancy will end in disaster. God knows everything, and we need to give Him our full and undivided trust.

Countless times, I've been getting to know someone and when I pray to God about him, He either comes to me in a dream or in my random thoughts with an answer. As of today, it has always been, "Nope, not him!" When I ignore his voice and continue the relationship, He reminds me in the interactions that I have with the guy about why He said no initially. This leads me to quickly dismissing the guy and apologizing to God for not listening sooner. I'm still growing in this area, but I'm thankful that I'm not the same as I used to be.

My old dating mindset was one of the moment. I looked for someone who was funny, good-looking, and easy to pass the time with. My standards were low and, in return, and I found myself spending my emotional resources on people that couldn't pour into my personal growth. Realizing that my time was precious and valuable became important to me, and I began to be more careful where I sowed my free time.

Connecting with people that can feed us emotionally, spiritually and mentally and stimulate our God-given gifts is wise when deciding which people to allow into our lives. When you are seeking a future life partner, consider the spirit that he carries. Do you want that spirit? (And vice versa.) A physical relationship will undoubtedly tie his spirit, good or bad, pleasant or ugly, to you. For example, I want someone who is kind and has a peaceful disposition that I can share. On the other hand, I don't want a liar or a manipulator. Those are both spirits I don't want any part of. On the flip side, I must make sure my own spirit is in check and positive so that my partner can gain a good spirit from me as well.

As people, we never stop growing, no matter our age, race, sex or even spiritual maturity. Always have it in the back of your mind that we are lifetime students, and nobody knows everything. During frustrating and complicated times or events, always know that all you're doing is learning. Embracing yourself as a student of Life University will ensure that you will always be evolving. Be open to making changes when needed and thrive on positivity and total dependence on God.

Every so often, I'll find myself leafing through old journals I used to keep from my late teens through to my late twenties. These old memoirs allow me to gauge the state my mind was in, and I can determine the difference in attitude and account for maturing. I saw a change in my relationships, faith, finances, recreational activities and even in the vocabulary I used (i.e. sailor mouth).

Develop a goal. Think about who and what you want to become. What type of women do you respect currently and why? I previously shared with you some famous and inspiring women of the Bible. We learned what they did and how they walked in their purpose. Make a list of the attributes of these women. This is called "mind mapping" when you're planning your new internal goals for who you want to become and how you are going to get there. Aim high in your thoughts because your creator thinks highly of you. I had an old friend who frequently used the phrase, "Reach for the starts and land on the moon." The ultimate product is to reach your full potential.

Jeremiah 29:11, KJV, states, *"For I know the thoughts that I think toward you, saith the LORD, thoughts of peace, and not of evil, to give you* *an* *expected end."* If God thinks highly of us, then we should think highly of ourselves as well.

Document, document, document. You will need a way of tracking your growth. You can use a notebook, journal, or even start a diary. You can also consider a vlog or blog that you make every couple of days, weekly, or monthly. Just so that after some time, you can go back and revisit old thoughts, feelings, and dramas. This will allow you to determine whether you have grown in certain areas of your life or that you need to work on them further. Not only do you keep these records for yourself, but also so you can offer a testimony to another woman who might need to hear your own personal experience. Personal mentors are just as influential as mentors who have a platform that we don't always have access to.

Regarding purity and documenting your growth will formally enable you to track the changes that you have subconsciously made: a shift in our mental paradigm will eventually make its way to our third dimension. Our subconscious is a powerful thing. This is how God speaks to us, where our feelings come from regarding ourselves and how we interact with the world around us. Fine tuning our fourth dimension

(known as our subconscious) and making sure it's in optimal condition will bring us closer to our creator. Sexual purity is a must for our prayer life and maximizes our potential for the plan God has for us. Abstinence and celibacy are not segregated into one aspect of life; it's a product that spills over into other areas as well, like finances, mental health and self-esteem. *"Therefore, if any man be in Christ, he is a new creature: old things are passed away; behold, all things are become new.*" — II Corinthians 5:17 KJV

***

April 2020

Dear Journal,

Whoa! It's been like a thousand years since the last time we chatted. My life has changed drastically, and I've experienced a million things. I feel like I need to catch you up on the major things that are going on right now and what I have accomplished. First, I'm not in touch with any of those old guys I used to deal with anymore. Yes, ma'am, I'm still in church every Sabbath. I also have a Sunday church that I attend regularly now as well. For the past couple of years or so, I kept feeling the Spirit leading me to attend a Sunday church, so I did. And I love it.

Their worship experience is like no other, and it's so crazy! I enjoy every minute of it, and the pastor is very encouraging. I've never been in services like the ones conducted there. It's a whole new learning experience for me, and I feel like my spiritual growth is going to another level. At my home church, I am part of different ministries:

hospitality, children's ministry, young adult ministry, and I was recently promoted to the assistant director's position for Community Services (my ultimate passion). By God's grace and mercy, I finally purchased my first starter home with cash a couple of years ago. It was a major upper, but I did most of the renovations (with God's help! lol) myself. It is not the Taj Mahal, but I am proud of it. My home is also PAID FOR! Praise be to God. Yes, I still foster kids from the state. I currently have 2 girls (unrelated); one is two, and the other is a couple of weeks old. I also graduated from a four-year university some years back, and I hold a bachelor's degree in science. I have been a practicing nurse for 10+ years. I've had the opportunity to be a travel nurse, and I spent about a year bouncing from state to state. Last spring, I felt the Spirit lead me to other avenues, this book being one of them.